"If
It V
You Want   "

He was offering her a fighting chance—the knowledge he had given her against his undisputed expertise.

The demon in her rose to the challenge. She couldn't resist the unspoken dare. "I appreciate the warning."

The deserted beach became the arena for the most primitive battle of all: man against woman. Frozen in the moment, the adversaries weighed each other's weaknesses, the slender golden girl and her towering dark-haired champion.

Then Brandon lowered his head, his mouth seeking and finding Summer's upturned lips. When the kiss ended, as it did abruptly when Summer drew away, they were both breathless.

Brandon's chest rose and fell quickly. "Now you know."

"Now I know," she echoed between breaths. She was fully aware that he had let her go when he could have held her in his embrace. The urge to return to his arms was strong. She could feel his silent command to surrender, but she resisted its siren call.

SARA CHANCE

is a "wife, mother, author—in that order," who currently resides in Florida with her husband. With the ocean only minutes from her front door, Ms. Chance enjoys both swimming and boating. *Her Golden Eyes* is Ms. Chance's first Silhouette Desire.

Dear Reader:

SILHOUETTE DESIRE is an exciting new line of contemporary romances from Silhouette Books. During the past year, many Silhouette readers have written in telling us what other types of stories they'd like to read from Silhouette, and we've kept these comments and suggestions in mind in developing SILHOUETTE DESIRE.

DESIREs feature all of the elements you like to see in a romance, plus a more sensual, provocative story. So if you want to experience all the excitement, passion and joy of falling in love, then SILHOUETTE DESIRE is for you.

I hope you enjoy this book and all the wonderful stories to come from SILHOUETTE DESIRE. I'd appreciate any thoughts you'd like to share with us on new SILHOUETTE DESIRE, and I invite you to write to us at the address below:

Karen Solem
Editor-in-Chief
Silhouette Books
P.O. Box 769
New York, N.Y. 10019

SARA CHANCE
Her Golden Eyes

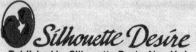

Silhouette Desire
Published by Silhouette Books New York
America's Publisher of Contemporary Romance

SILHOUETTE BOOKS, a Simon & Schuster Division of
GULF & WESTERN CORPORATION
1230 Avenue of the Americas, New York, N.Y. 10020

Copyright © 1983 by Sydney Ann Clary

Distributed by Pocket Books

ISBN: 0-671-46349-7

First Silhouette Books printing February, 1983

10 9 8 7 6 5 4 3 2 1

SILHOUETTE, SILHOUETTE DESIRE and colophon are
trademarks of Simon & Schuster.

America's Publisher of Contemporary Romance

Printed in the U.S.A.

Her
Golden Eyes

1

~~~~~~~~~~~~~~~~

Rain, driven by gusty winds, lashed the windows of the two-storied houseboat, buffeting the huge structure until it strained at its moorings. It was actually too spacious to answer to the term houseboat, being more of a floating home resting on top of a large rectangular barge moored in a small cove on the south side of the Florida inlet. "The Nest," as it was affectionately called, the boat dock that ran alongside it, the small bait and tackle store on the beach and the charter boat *Sea Mist* made up the business complex known as Tom's Rest.

It was well past midnight, but the lights in The Nest were still burning. Summer McAllister was on her weekly shift for Rescue Radio, a project started by her late husband, Tom.

Manned by volunteers, the organization provided 'round-the-clock monitoring of the VHF emergency channel. Countless boats and personnel owed their lives to the men and women who donated their time, money and equipment to relay distress messages to the Coast Guard and, in many cases, render on-the-spot assistance.

Summer glanced over her shoulder at the sliding glass doors leading to the sun porch. The rain battered the dark expanse as the winds rose to a mournful howl. The lighthouse across the inlet was a blurred shadow as it made its sweeping arc of light across the Atlantic, warning marine craft of the reef that lay just offshore. Although the Florida coastline appeared to be smooth and sandy, coral reefs waited just below the surface in silent menace to rip the bottoms of unwary boats.

Summer turned back with a sigh to the quarterly sales tax report she had been working on while she kept her lonely vigil. A small calculator lay at her right elbow on top of the radio logbook. Resignedly, she eyed the long column of figures waiting to be totaled. This was one of the times she missed Tom's quiet presence. She hated paperwork, and since his death her evenings seemed filled with it. How often had she kept him company beside a silent radio doing exactly this. The chore had gone so much faster with two to share it.

She couldn't have got along without Gussie's help, she acknowledged fairly. Alone, she knew she would have had a much harder time coping. She picked up her pencil, determined to finish the tedious job before morning. One good thing about bad weather—there was little chance of interruptions. The small-craft warnings had all except the huge freighters scurrying for safe harbors.

She bent her curly head and concentrated on the papers in front of her. She carefully punched out the entries of the weekly receipts from the bait store, the dockage charges and the charter fees on the calculator. It was nearly an hour later before she leaned back in the creaky captain's chair and gave a sigh of satisfaction. The tax report lay signed and sealed in its envelope in the outgoing mail basket.

"I've earned a rest, Sailor," she announced quietly to the gray shaggy mongrel on the floor beside her chair.

The dog opened one dark eye in response to her voice and thumped his tail against the edge of the desk.

"Such enthusiasm," she grinned as she stood up, stretching lazily like a sleek golden cat.

Feline was the best way to describe Summer's five-foot-seven-inch form. Topped by a tawny mass of sun-bleached honey curls, her slender, long-legged body was tanned a light bronze from countless hours on the open sea. Although she was months past her twenty-eighth birthday, her figure was still as lithe and firm as any teenager despite having borne a daughter. Perhaps her most outstanding feature was her slanted amber eyes framed by thick sable lashes.

Summer moved silently across the room to the kitchen to plug in the coffee pot Gussie had left prepared for her on the counter. While she waited for it to perk, she set out a brown earthenware mug and a plate of Gussie's cookies.

"I hope Shannon hasn't counted these," she mused aloud. She leaned against the counter and bit into the sugar wafer, thinking about her daughter. In two days she would be eight years old. It didn't seem possible. Where had the time gone?

It was five years since Tom had died, she realized with a sense of shock—since she had become a single parent and sole owner of Tom's Rest.

The red light on the pot signaled the brew was finished. She filled her cup and carried it and the plate of cookies back to the radio. She sat down, propped her denim-clad legs up on the desk and cradled the mug in her hands. The wind howled forlornly, making her glad she was dry and indoors. The weather report had said the seas would run about eight to ten feet. A nasty night for anybody to be out. She sipped her black coffee carefully, enjoying the relative silence of the house. The rhythmic roll of the boat at its moorings was soothing, though much more pronounced than usual.

Suddenly the quiet was pierced by a deep male voice.

"This is Whiskey Zulu X-ray 8478 vessel *Shalimar* calling CG station Lake Worth."

Instantly alert, Summer gave her attention to the disembodied voice. "This is CG station Lake Worth . . . vessel *Shalimar*. We copy you . . . switch to channel twenty-two and transmit."

Summer flipped her selector, noting the time and a short description in her logbook as she did so.

". . . be advised have lost power . . . am taking on water . . . request a tow . . . My position is . . . Am drifting northward approximately three knots . . . about two miles offshore."

". . . be advised we have a boat underway for a tow . . . will arrive approximately one and a half hours . . . repeat will arrive one and a half hours . . . Can you stay afloat?"

". . . Am pumping now . . . best estimate one hour."

Summer picked up her mike. She didn't need the map on the wall in front of her to pinpoint the disabled craft.

"Vessel *Shalimar*, this is Jupiter Rescue Tango George Sam 3873. We have been monitoring your transmission. May we be of assistance? Over."

She waited, her pencil poised to record the vessel's response in her log. Clearly, help was needed now. The same voice responded almost before she finished transmitting. One tiny portion of her mind noted its rich, smooth cadences even as she concentrated on his answer.

"We are in need of immediate assistance . . . seas are

increasing . . . taking on water rapidly in spite of our pumps . . . How long before you can reach us . . . over."

"Our estimated time is thirty minutes. Will be off air waves ten minutes while we get underway. Will contact you as soon as possible . . . over."

"We copy . . . over."

Summer quickly dialed Joe, her first mate. While the phone rang she finished logging the necessary details about the rescue ahead. As soon as she heard Joe's sleepy voice, she gave her orders.

"Meet me at the boat, three minutes. We've got a run," she announced tersely. She hung up on his brief "Okay" and grabbed her rainsuit from the peg by the door.

She struggled into the jacket as she hurried to her aunt's bedroom. Being a light sleeper, Augusta was awake at Summer's light touch. Accustomed to the middle-of-the-night summons, she sat up alertly.

"We have a run," Summer whispered in the darkness. There was no need to wake the child who slept in the room next door. "It's recorded in the log. Joe's on his way."

The faint groan of mattress springs indicated Gussie had reached for the robe she kept on the chair near the bed. "I'll have coffee waiting," she answered calmly with equal brevity. Extra words wasted precious seconds.

Summer nodded, forgetting her aunt couldn't see her in the darkened room, before she turned and headed for the door. She paused just long enough to step into her protective vinyl pants before braving the rain-lashed night.

Seconds later she hit the planks of the *Sea Mist's* dock at a dead run. Behind her she heard Joe's door slam as he, too, raced for the thirty-one-foot *Bertram*.

11

The *Sea Mist,* tethered fore and aft, rode the angry water like a wild mare, tossing and bucking in the teeth of the wind-driven rain. Hesitating only to time her leap, Summer landed cat-footed on the open rear deck. Knowing Joe would get the lines, she went straight to the cockpit and started the engines.

The inlet, notoriously tricky to navigate, was doubly treacherous in this weather. Their lives depended on the performance of their craft. The engines throbbed to life on the first try. She listened attentively to their purr as she switched on the running lights and the radio.

A sudden thud followed by the boat's swift rocking told her Joe was on board. She glanced over her shoulder.

"Ready?" she shouted against the screeching storm. They'd done this so many times they were a smooth working team.

"Yeah!" Joe roared back. He held the remaining line in his hands, waiting for Summer's signal to cast off.

She eased the boat out of neutral. "Let her go," she yelled without turning around. She concentrated on guiding the *Sea Mist* between the huge piling and the dock toward the open water. Once free of the mooring area she pushed the throttle forward, feeling the boat surge underfoot.

Joe joined her in the comparative shelter of the cockpit. His faded eyes squinted in concentration on the narrow channel ahead. The white-crested waves showed up clearly in the inky darkness, and the ominous roar of their assault on the rocky jetties lining both sides of the inlet warned that the *Sea Mist* passage was hazardous if not downright foolhardy.

"Get on the radio, Joe. The craft is *Shalimar,*" she ordered curtly. She steadied *Sea Mist's* plunging progress by adjusting the power. Ahead was the long line of white foam indicating the sandbar blocking the inlet's exit. She was dimly conscious of Joe's voice as he obtained the *Shalimar's* new position. She braced her legs against the console and threw her weight into the wheel, forcing the *Sea Mist* hard to starboard into the narrow channel path along the south beach. It was the only safe way out. The bow slashed through the ten-foot waves, showering salt spray in all directions. Unprotected now by land, the boat rose high on each new roller to plunge sickeningly down into the next trough.

"You need to correct about two degrees more to the south," Joe advised at her elbow.

She nodded, already swinging the wheel to make the adjustment.

"How's he doing?" she asked.

"Not too bad, considering. Says he thinks he hit something and popped a strut. Messed up both propellers."

Summer peered into the gloom, searching for a telltale sign of light. It was too soon, she knew. Yet many a time a disabled vessel was closer in than first thought.

"Got three passengers aboard, two women and another man. Nobody hurt."

"Good. If he has his position right, we should be seeing his lights in about ten minutes."

Joe peered anxiously through the rain-splattered windshield. "Can't be much farther out. The Gulf Stream must be murder. God help him and us if he drifts into that."

Summer nodded in agreement. "I know. Did you tell him to send up a flare when he sighted us?"

"Uh-huh," he grunted as the *Sea Mist* rolled into the valley between two huge waves.

Neither Summer nor her mate appeared to notice the

wall of water on either side of them. When the boat powered up to the crest of the next roller, they searched again for their quarry.

A tiny pinpoint of light flickered ahead. "Do you see it? About ten degrees port?" she asked.

Seconds passed while they waited for the beam to appear again.

"Now I do," Joe rumbled, reaching for the mike. "This is *Sea Mist* calling *Shalimar*. Do you copy? Over."

An excited voice responded immediately. "This is *Shalimar*. We read you. Over."

Summer's quick ear caught the Yankee twang in the man's speech. This had to be the other male passenger.

Joe spoke again. "We have you in sight. Fire a flare for confirmation. Over."

"Will do."

Seconds later the pitch-black sky was split by a burst of red fire.

"Now for the hard stuff," Joe muttered before he pressed the mike's transmitter button. "We are going to make a swing by your stern from port to starboard to toss a line. Over."

"Got it," came back the answer.

"Gawd! I hope the guy catching the line is more of a seaman than this joker." His disgust was evident. "Dumb fool. Why don't these Sunday boaters use a bathtub for their playing."

Joe's ill-humored tirade brought a grin to Summer's lips. "You can tear a strip off the captain if you like," she offered. "*After* we get home!"

"Humph," he grunted.

Summer's hands were busy as she swung her smaller craft into position for the first run at the wallowing cruiser. "Get ready, Joe," she ordered automatically. Timing the swells and the wind force, she moved into position. "Here we go," she shouted as she eased the throttle forward to plunge down the wave at an angle to the cruiser. She didn't look back to see whether Joe was prepared. She didn't need to. Right now her job was to keep the boats from colliding as the *Sea Mist* passed within a few feet of *Shalimar's* stern.

"Damn it, I missed," Joe bellowed. "Try again, a little closer."

Again Summer maneuvered into position, only this time she slid dangerously near to *Shalimar's* sleek hull. For a brief second she pulled back on the gas to slow her progress, giving Joe extra time to make his cast.

"Got it!"

She popped the throttle forward quickly as *Shalimar* rolled drunkenly toward them.

"It's secure to the bow," the Yankee voice announced over the radio.

Joe was beside her again. "I'll take it," he offered, picking up the mike to answer.

"Good," she replied. Her job required all her concentration. Easing forward carefully to take up the slack between the boats, she felt the drag on the *Sea Mist's* powerful engine when it took on the dead weight of the *Shalimar*. Then she began a wide arc back to the inlet through which she had come.

The return trip took much longer. By the time the white frothing of the sandbar was in sight, Summer's shoulders and legs ached with tension and the buffeting of the ocean.

"Shorten the line, Joe," she commanded tersely. She was more worried than she cared to admit by the floundering vessel in her wake. It took all her strength to hold the lighter *Sea Mist* on course. There was very little margin for error once they entered the narrow channel along the beach and the inlet beyond.

"Done it," he mouthed against her ear, anxiety making him careful not to spoil her concentration. He watched admiringly while she threaded the slender eye of the needle leading to safety. Gawd! She was her father all over again, young as she was.

"Good job," he said approvingly when they had passed the critical point.

Summer acknowledged his compliment with a relieved grin. "See if Gussie alerted Kevin, would you? I'll take them right to his marina."

"Sure." He raised Gussie without any trouble. "She says Kevin called a few minutes ago from the office. The cradle is down in the water waiting for us." He glanced over his shoulder. "Bet that guy's glad we were around."

Summer guided the *Sea Mist* toward the long gas dock of the marina with the *Shalimar* now snubbed close. Joe left his place to man the towline, shortening it so that the *Shalimar* was eased gently into position. Summer cut the engine before moving onto the dock to secure her boat. She knew Joe and Kevin between them would be able to swing the other craft into place over the marine railway cradle that would haul the *Shalimar* safely ashore. Summer straightened and blew on her icy fingers to warm them. The storm was easing, but the rain streamed down her face, some of it trickling inside her jacket despite the snugly tied drawstring hood. She was cold and damp, her deck shoes soaked. She longed for her bed, but there were still the passengers to see to. She jammed her hands in her pockets and headed for the *Shalimar*.

The lights of the marina cast an eerie glow over the yellow-slickered men working alongside the disabled craft. Summer recognized Joe's stocky bulk and Kevin's bare head at the port side fore and aft.

"Hold her steady," someone shouted from the starboard stern.

Summer couldn't see the owner of the velvet voice, hidden as he was by the *Shalimar*.

"Damn it, shorten the line, Chuck," the voice roared as a wave caught the boat, pushing it out of position.

Summer halted under the overhang of the control shed to stay out of the way. Her position gave her an excellent view of the whole operation. Luckily the wind was letting up.

"Tie it off," Kevin yelled as the *Shalimar* finally came to rest against the supporting cradle.

Summer's eyes were trained on the tall figure farthest away. There was something about him that drew her interest. She nodded approvingly when he smoothly obeyed Kevin's command. Obviously, he was no Sunday sailor. She hurried across to lend a hand, passing Kevin on the way.

"Rotten night, Summer," he observed, raking his hand through his wet hair.

She grinned. "You should see outside," she teased, using the fisherman's slang for the ocean before adding seriously, "Hold off before pulling her out. There are two women still aboard."

"Okay, Cap'n. Holler when you're ready."

Joe was alone on the dock when she joined him. The other two men were already on board collecting their gear.

"Aren't you going to help?" she asked as she swung onto the deck herself.

"Owner asked me to stay here to get the ladies off," he grunted, his shoulders hunched against the weather. At least the rain had let up.

"Are you sure the boat's tied up, Amy? We're safe?" The female voice trembled with traces of lingering panic. "Why can't we get off? What's taking so long?"

17

Summer pushed open the door and stepped into the plush salon. She saw two women seated on the sofa directly in front of her. The younger one, a brunette, held a small glass, which Summer guessed to be brandy.

"Here, drink this, Joyce," the dark-haired girl commanded.

"May I help?" Summer asked, seeing the telltale pallor of fear and shock on both faces.

Both women glanced toward her. "Who are you?" the girl called Joyce demanded.

Summer's brow raised at the rude question, but she didn't retaliate. She saw the girl's shaking hands as she raised the brandy to her lips. Compassion softened her voice. "I came to see if I could do anything," she explained quietly. "Joe is outside waiting to help you both ashore. You'll feel much better on land."

"You're a woman!" Joyce gasped, surprise momentarily driving out the fear from her near brush with disaster.

"Why, thank you," Summer responded with a grin in the girl's direction. "I don't know how you can tell." She tried to ease the emotional tension in the confined space. Both women needed to unwind after their ordeal.

Amy liked the golden-eyed girl almost on sight. She had not missed the flash of anger at Joyce's rudeness, yet she had not responded in kind. "Is he the captain?" she asked. "We all owe our lives to him."

"Actually, he's—" Summer began, only to be interrupted by the two men entering the cabin.

Summer's eyes widened in stunned recognition of the taller of the two. Brandon Marshall! There was no mistaking that often photographed, handsome face.

His usual let-me-get-to-know-you-better smile was absent as he stared at the blonde. "I thought I told you to get into your raincoat. You too, Amy," he added, turning to the other woman. Glancing in Summer's direction, he thrust the duffel bag and suitcase he carried into her hands. "Take these for me, son," he ordered.

Summer raised an eyebrow at his abrupt command, then shrugged as she obeyed. Right now it was important to get the boat out of the water. She could hardly blame him for his curt manners considering the shape of his cruiser. She knew how she would feel if it were the *Sea Mist*.

Brandon caught his girlfriend's arm and drew her to her feet. "Let's go. There are two men outside in the rain waiting for us to get out of their way." He glanced over his shoulder to see Chuck and Summer still there. "I'll bring the girls. You two go on."

Summer swung the duffel over her shoulder and followed his friend to the deck. Behind her she could hear Joyce.

"You're pulling my arm, Brand," she complained. "Believe me, I want to get off this precious boat of yours, so let go!"

Once outside, Summer stood aside while Chuck assisted Amy across to the dock. But Joyce was another matter. She took one look at the narrow gap of black, churning water between the deck and the pier and shrieked in protest.

"I won't jump that!" she cried, clutching at Brandon's arms.

"Of course you will," he replied, his jaw rigid with exasperation. "It's the only way to get ashore. Amy did it." He held the struggling girl firmly by the shoulders. "Now come on. I'll hold your hand while you step up here." He patted the foot threads on the gunwale. "Then when I say jump, you jump. Chuck and Joe will catch you."

"It's not as bad as it looks," Amy called encouragingly.

"No, I can't! I can't!" Joyce backed against Brandon, her head shaking from side to side.

"Damn!" he swore, his temper finally snapped. "Of all the stupid—" He swallowed the rest of his anger and swept the blonde into his arms. "You better hold on," he ordered. He poised, testing his balance for a second, then leaped, landing safely on the dock. He wasted no time in putting his burden down.

As she picked up the duffel, Summer bent her head to hide her amusement at his obvious disgust. She was willing to bet this was one woman who wasn't going to be around long.

"Take the girls on over to the office while I help with the baggage," Brandon directed before turning his attention to Summer. "Toss it over, son."

Son? Damn the man. If he called her son one more time! For a split second she considered slinging the bag as hard as she could at him. Then she quashed the thought. He looked big enough to withstand the shock. One part of her mind appraised him as she underhanded the canvas sack.

He was tall, at least six feet three inches, and apparently extremely fit. Tanned, too; sunlamp or authentic, it didn't matter. He was still attractive. And those eyes! Bedroom eyes, she recalled one gossip columnist had dubbed them. They were the color of sunlit sea—aquamarine, with tiny flicks of burnished gold. Except for the betraying silver wings in his sable brown hair at each temple, he could easily have passed for less than the thirty-eight he was. He was every inch the rich international darling.

"Now you!"

The abrupt command startled her, making her realize she'd been staring. She pulled herself together quickly, annoyed by the awareness growing in her. Without a word she mounted the gunwale and jumped lightly across the narrow gap, landing beside Joe. He picked up Chuck's two cases, leaving Brandon to carry what was left.

"I'm going to check with Kevin," she murmured to her mate. "I'll see you back at the boat." At Joe's nod, she headed for the control shack. Behind her she heard Marshall question Joe about transportation. She was out of earshot before he replied.

"How's it doing?" she asked as she stepped inside the control room.

Kevin looked over his shoulder briefly. "Okay. I'll have her high and dry in a sec." His hands moved surely over the multidial panel. He kept his eyes trained on the dark shape inching its way out of the water. "She's a beauty."

Summer nodded in appreciation, her gaze drawn to the sleek lines of the thirty-seven-foot boat. "Is it ever!" The craft, a Rybovich, and its owner had a lot in common. Both were aristocrats with long lineages of breeding. She tugged the strings of her rainhood and slipped it off her head before unzipping her jacket. Outside the rain had finally stopped.

Kevin cut the switch. "Done. Let's go see the damage," he suggested. He pointed to the tall figure striding to the *Shalimar's* stern. "Looks like the owner has the same idea."

"If she were mine, I would, too," Summer agreed, walking beside him across the asphalt workyard to where the disabled *Shalimar* waited.

As they drew nearer, the underside of the cruiser was plainly visible from the ground level as the craft lay cradled in the wood supports of the railway lift. The bent shaft and damaged props were self-explanatory.

"It must have been a damn log." The muttered curse

sounded from the offside. Summer moved around the stern with Kevin to get a better view of the damage.

Brandon Marshall was down on his haunches, checking the extent of the destruction. He looked up, catching sight of her for the first time. His eyes narrowed assessingly, taking in the tousled honey curls and the slender womanly curves revealed through her open jacket.

Even in the dim light Summer read his appreciation. Usually she was immune to such blatant interest, but not this time. Something about this man provoked an answering response. She watched as he rose slowly to his feet.

"I didn't realize Kevin had brought someone with him," he explained with an easy smile. "Sorry about getting him out at this time of night."

Behind her, Summer heard the marina owner splutter. She grinned, imagining Madge's reaction if she caught her husband keeping a woman on the side. She'd kill her first, then him. Her Italian temper wouldn't be satisfied with anything less. "Sorry to disappoint you, but I didn't come with Kevin," she replied.

His brow quirked in puzzlement.

"She's the captain of the *Sea Mist*," Kevin snapped. He hadn't missed the gleam of speculation in the other man's eyes, and he didn't like it. Summer had grown up on the docks, and they all were protective of her. There was no way this Yankee tourist was going to insult her while he was around.

"The *Sea Mist?*" Brandon asked, obviously not making the connection.

Summer turned slightly, pointing to her boat lying alongside the dock. She saw him stiffen as the full implication hit.

"You're the captain? You piloted that boat out there?" he demanded sharply.

"Afraid so," she admitted.

"You're the one I spoke to on the radio?"

"Right again."

Brandon stared at her intently, taking in her smile and the easy way she stood his scrutiny. A woman! Many men, he knew, would have backed down from what she had done. It was a humbling thought to know he had been brought in by a female.

Summer studied him as carefully as he did her. It didn't take much intelligence to guess at what was going through his mind. No captain liked the idea of being towed in, and most definitely not by a girl. If he ran true to form, he would do one of two things—either be mad as hell or sickeningly patronizing.

He did neither. He held out his hand in a gesture of acceptance and equality.

Surprised, Summer placed hers in his grasp.

"It was a damned nice job. Thank you," he said simply.

She searched his face, looking for some sign of mockery. There was none. He meant it. She nodded mutely, embarrassed by her negative preconceptions.

Kevin, a silent onlooker, found his opinion of the Yankee going up. At least he knew quality when he saw it. Unknowingly, he came to Summer's rescue. "Look, if you get your stuff together, I'll drop you and your group by the Hilton on my way home," he suggested.

Brandon reluctantly let go of Summer's fine-boned hand. He glanced at the older man. "Good idea. The women will appreciate it, I know."

"I'll get Joe, then we'll be on our way," Summer said.

Kevin reached in his pocket for his keys. "It will only take a minute to lock up, then I'll meet you at the office."

Brandon fell into step beside her as they crossed the asphalt work area. He leaned across her to open the marina's back door. The spill of light from inside caught the dull gold gleam of her wedding band. His hand on her shoulder stopped her when she would have preceded him.

"Doesn't your husband care about what you're doing? Why doesn't he handle this sort of thing himself?" he demanded.

Summer frowned at his odd questions. "Tom?"

"If that's his name. Doesn't he care that you've been out there risking your neck?" His low-toned voice was harsh.

Summer's eyes darkened in a flare of resentment. What business was it of his, what she did? He should be grateful she had responded to his distress call instead of tearing away at Tom.

"My husband is dead," she stated coldly. "But even if he weren't, I'd still have been in that boat tonight." Pride forbade her telling him Tom would have been its captain.

He went still as her words sunk in. "I'm sorry," he apologized slowly.

Summer inclined her head with a stiff nod. "If you will excuse me . . ." She whipped quickly past him into Kevin's office.

"Ready to go, Summer?" Joe asked, placing his empty coffee mug on the edge of the desk he had been leaning against. Noticing Summer's rigid stance, he glanced appraisingly at the man behind her.

"I am," she answered flatly. Turning to leave, Summer found herself brought up short against Brandon's long frame. She tipped her head back to look up at him.

"Summer, I—" he began, his eyes on her cool expression. Unconsciously he had used the name her mate had given.

"Brand, please, can't we leave this place?" Joyce wailed. "I want a bath. I want to get warm again!"

Brandon looked impatiently toward her huddled form, exasperation plain in his expression. He raked his fingers through his hair at the pleading look on her pale face. "All right, in a minute," he sighed.

"Now!" she demanded, remnants of her experience making her voice sharp.

He turned angrily to Joyce, his momentary softening dispelled by her command.

Seeing her chance while he was distracted by his girlfriend, Summer slipped by.

"Good luck with the *Shalimar*," she called as she stepped outside. She glanced over her shoulder to see him watching her walk away. She couldn't read his expression, but she felt the impact of his stare. For a second she knew the stirring of forgotten desire. She shrugged in confused anger at the unlooked-for response. It wasn't likely she would ever see him again, she decided, turning to follow Joe's comfortable bulk back to the *Sea Mist*.

2

Brandon Marshall entered the tackle store and glanced around appreciatively. So far this morning he had visited three such places, but this was the most attractive of the lot. From the outside its rough-textured exterior blended perfectly with the towering Australian pines surrounding it.

Inside it was clean, with only a mild trace of the usually strong bait smell. The displays of new equipment as well as the array of favorite standbys indicated the knowledge and expertise of its owner. It was no wonder the place had come so highly recommended in spite of its smaller size.

"May I help you, sir?"

Brandon gazed at the tiny gray-haired lady behind the counter. Her soft drawl reminded him of the girl last night. "I'm looking for Captain McAllister. I understand it might be possible to charter his boat for two weeks?"

Gussie frowned slightly. "That depends on when you want to go," she explained. "This is our busiest season."

"I know all that," he agreed wearily. He was beginning to think this trip was jinxed. It was hard to believe every competent captain was already spoken for. "I want a boat for the next two weeks. My own is in the shop as of last night. I was told you might be able to help me."

At the mention of the date, Gussie brightened. "Maybe we can at that. One of our regular charters has cancelled—"

"I'll take it," Brandon announced before she could finish.

'It's a two-weeker at Treasure Cay in the Bahamas, but it doesn't begin for three more days," she warned. "Plus there are no overnight accommodations since it's a thirty-one-foot open layout. You'll need hotel reservations unless you want to take the ones that go with the charter."

Brandon nodded. "I'll take them."

Gussie reached for the charter book lying open beside the cash register. She crossed out Fletcher's party, then looked up. "Your name, please?"

"Brandon Marshall," he replied, watching idly. He saw her start of surprise.

"You're the man Summer towed in?" she exclaimed.

His puzzlement at her comment showed. "You know her?"

She nodded with a smile. "Summer is my sister-in-law."

"Is she around? I never got to thank her."

"Today she is. The weather was too bad to go out." She quickly penned in his name, then glanced across the room.

"Shannon."

Brandon followed her eyes. A small child of eight or nine sat on a crate in one corner. She was petite, with a

27

mop of sunshine curls framing a delicate face. Her navy shorts and red striped tee-shirt gave her a bouncy air of mischief. She looked up at the older woman's call.

"Would you take Mr. Marshall down to the *Sea Mist?*"

At the mention of the familiar name a vague thought began to form in Brandon's mind.

The girl slid from her seat, placing the box of hooks she was separating on the crate. "Sure," she agreed with a grin, coming over to them.

"Shannon will show you the way." Gussie picked up a printed sheet and passed it to him. "These are some tips we give all our customers. It should answer any questions you may have."

He thanked her and turned to follow his guide out the back of the shop.

The child led the way down the smooth, pine-needled path to the dock. "You don't live here, do you?" she asked, eyeing him curiously.

He looked down at her small face, intrigued by the almost adult certainty in her voice. "No, I come from up north."

Her green eyes widened. "You don't sound it."

He chuckled outright. "Maybe not, but I do. Do you live here?" he asked.

"Mm-hmm." She pointed to the large floating home moored in the shallows of the inlet to their right. "Over there."

"Nice."

"Is it ever. The kids at school are always bugging me to invite them over," she confided in a rush.

"And do you?"

"Sometimes," she shrugged. "With Mom busy like she is, I try not to make more work."

"I'm sure she appreciates it," he observed carefully.

Mentally he condemned the unknown mother. Didn't working women ever stop to consider what their jobs did to their families?

"Here we are," Shannon announced and hopped onto the deck of the *Sea Mist*. She glanced back at her companion. "Why are you standing there? Come aboard."

Brandon shook his head. "No, I'll stay here. The captain might not like it . . ."

"Shannon, is that you?" Summer stuck her head out of the cabin door. "You're supposed to be helping Gussie."

"I am. She sent me down with a customer." She pointed to the dock.

Summer's gaze followed her gesture to meet aquamarine eyes in startled silence.

Brandon studied her as she came toward him. Without the concealing stiffness of her yellow slicker she was a sleek, almost sensual animal. Her sun-kissed skin, untouched by cosmetics, gleamed with health. As she came closer he could she her strange golden eyes. She was probably the most primitively attractive woman he had ever seen. Her basic earthiness touched some fount of male need. Civilization and all its polish dissolved beneath his sudden urge to stake a claim on the glowingly alive female before him. Shannon's childish voice brought him back to the present century.

"He's taking over your charter with Mr. Fletcher to the Bahamas, Mom. 'Cause Mrs. Fletcher's not up to coming this year," Shannon announced, dropping the proverbial bombshell as only a child can.

"My charter?"

"Your mother?"

Both adults stared at Shannon, their surprise and shock evident even to her young eyes. "What's wrong?" she asked, bewildered. "I thought you'd be pleased, Mom." She turned to Brandon. "You said you wanted Captain McAllister, didn't you?"

Summer took a deep breath and let it out in a sigh. "Look, honey, why don't you go on back to the store? Gussie will be needing you. I'm just surprised, that's all."

Her daughter's glance flickered across her face before settling on the tall man still on the dock.

He nodded, adding his assurance. "I didn't realize your mother was the captain I signed with, Shannon."

"Everyone around here knows she's the captain," Shannon stated indignantly, her small fists planted on her hips. "Daddy said she was as good as him. Joe says so, too."

"Shannon!" Summer interjected quickly. "That's enough."

Her daughter turned to her. "Well, he did," she asserted, not prepared to back down an inch on what she considered to be a slur against her mother and her ability.

Summer understood her child's need to defend her and it showed in the soft look in her eyes. "That's not the point, honey. You're being rude. Apologize, please."

Defiant green eyes clashed with gold until finally the bright blond curls bobbed slowly. "I'm sorry if I was ugly," she offered with quiet dignity.

Although Brandon had had little to do with children, he was impressed by the obvious affection between the two. Even Shannon's outspokenness was forgivable— in a way, even admirable. He stepped across to the *Sea Mist's* deck, then knelt down so he was on Shannon's level. He smiled into her wide-eyed gaze. "If I ever have a little girl, I hope she loves me enough to take up for me like you did for your mother. Caring like that is never ugly. Blunt, yes. But not ugly."

He raised his eyes to Summer. He read her watchful expression, the suspicion lurking in the molten honey stare.

Summer gazed at him, caught in the demanding fire of his eyes. His gentleness with Shannon baffled her. It didn't fit well with his playboy image. Again she felt the stirrings of interest too long denied. It was difficult to tear her eyes away from his handsome face, but she managed, just. She turned to her daughter.

"Gussie will be wondering where you got to," she scolded, pleased that her voice didn't betray her awareness of the man still on one knee on her deck.

"Aw, Mom, can't I stay here?" she protested. "It's no fun sortin' hooks."

Somehow the often repeated childish complaint reassured Summer. The fine tension in her body melted and she grinned at Shannon's disgust. "No, you can't if you want to go out with us tomorrow."

The defeated shrug of her daughter's shoulders said it all as she climbed slowly back onto the dock. Her plodding walk was an eloquent picture of her feelings, which lasted all of a half dozen steps. Then she turned, smiled widely and waved. "Nice to meet you, Mr. Marshall," she called before skipping off.

Brandon stood up and brushed his knees. His attempt to suppress his amusement at the child's antics was only partially successful.

Summer saw the twitch of his lips. Suddenly the laughter she, too, controlled bubbled to the surface, destroying Brandon's reserve. They collapsed in the deck chairs at the stern of the boat and gave way to their mirth. For a moment the attraction between them altered with this sharing of laughter. Their smiles slowly died as their eyes met and held.

31

Brandon was conscious of the rapid rise and fall of the taut breasts lovingly covered by a yellow tee-shirt, the long, slender legs stretched below the cut-off denim shorts. He knew an insane urge to grasp those slender shoulders and cover that lush mouth with his. "Is she always like that?" he asked, barely aware of his question, only knowing the need to prolong the moment of contact.

"She's an imp, all right," Summer acknowledged in a husky murmur. The intensity of his eyes was an almost tangible caress. Unknowingly she swayed toward him. Nerve endings tingled with bewildering sensations. She swallowed, feeling suddenly nervous and out of her depth. This man had a worldwide reputation for seduction if the gossip reporters were to be believed. Was she to be another one in a long list of conquests? His words were innocent enough, but heavens, the look in his eyes sure as hell wasn't. Bedroom eyes! It was worse than that. Wide, deserted beaches, whispering palms, erotic dreamy nights slumbered in those sea-green depths.

When the warmth of his lips touched hers it was an extension of the sensuous fantasy her mind had created. Lightly teasing, softly beguiling, his mouth seduced a response before she had time to resist. Her lips softened under his delicate touch. When his tongue extended his exploration Summer came out of her daydream with a jolt. Jerking away from his intoxicating hold on her lips, Summer stared at him in shock. Never in her life had she known such an instant response to a man. She tried to read the calm stillness of his expression, but she failed. He neither spoke or made any effort to repeat what had just happened. He simply sat watching her intently as though she were a puzzle he needed to solve.

Mentally she shook herself free of his spell. "Are you

really interested in taking the Fletchers' charter?" she asked, seizing gratefully on the purpose of his visit.

Brandon sensed her withdrawal and wondered at it. She was no innocent virgin to be frightened of a man's admiration. Was there someone else in her life? No sign of his curiosity showed as he accepted the change of subject. "I am. There will be a party of four, including me."

The mention of Joyce and the other couple with him somehow snapped her out of her bewildering thoughts. She was a fool to read so much into a kiss. Obviously the blonde still had his interest.

"Are you after anything in particular?" Summer could have bitten her tongue over the phrasing of her question. He wasn't one to miss the possibilities. She stared straight at him, daring him to make a comment.

The knowing look in his eye told her he followed her thoughts. Yet his words again were innocent of innuendo. "I hope we catch some kingfish. If not, then we'll settle for wahoo or snapper. Chuck swears he wants a white marlin, even if Amy doesn't." He grinned, remembering Amy's comment about trophy fishing when Chuck had voiced his ambition during the trip down. Seeing Summer's questioning expression, he explained, "I'm afraid Chuck's wife doesn't think too much of keeping what you don't eat."

"I can understand her point of view," she agreed. "I'm not fond of trophy hunters myself." She met his gaze unflinchingly, willing him to take the hint. Two weeks in the close confines of the *Sea Mist* with these electric charges between them, and especially with a jealous girlfriend along, were not appealing.

Brandon caught the message. She warned him off. Until that moment he had not seriously considered actively pursuing her. The challenge in her golden stare changed his mind. This woman was a worthy adversary. Not only did she attract him physically, but her very assurance was also a provocative dare against his manhood. She was a wild creature he felt a strong desire to tame. A predatory gleam lit his eyes for a split second, turning them to jade. "That depends on the trophy, surely."

Summer found Brandon's words echoing in her mind the next day. In fact, he invaded her thoughts too often. The look of him, the velvet stroke of his voice, the touch of his lips were as clear as the sun overhead. She glanced up at the blinding white ball.

"Why don't you go away," she muttered aloud.

"Are you crazy, girl?" Joe demanded from the dock. He dropped the coil of line he carried on the wood planking. A royal blue duffel bag was tucked under one arm while he carried two custom boat rods wrapped in matching blue tones in the other. "The last thing we need is rain. Wasn't last night enough for you?"

Was it ever! she thought wryly. If you only knew! She ignored his comment. "Good grief, Joe, are you moving in?" she demanded as she crossed over to take the rods.

"Don't be an idiot. Does this look like my stuff?" he asked in disgust.

Summer couldn't help laughing, knowing his opinion of color-coordinated tackle. "Let me guess. Jamieson, right?"

"Yup," he grunted. "Since I'm in the neighborhood, I thought I'd drop off my equipment." His mimic of the bored but wealthy charter of the next morning was uncanny down to the man's precise walk.

Summer stowed the expensive fiberglass beauties carefully. "Well, at least they aren't pink and gold."

"Gawd." Her mate rolled his eyes heavenward. "Give me strength. That woman. It's a wonder she

34

didn't dye her hair pink," he said, remembering their most eccentric client.

Summer took the duffel and headed for the cabin. "Did Gussie tell you Fletcher isn't coming this year?" she called over her shoulder.

"Yeah, she said that guy we hauled in came by about noon to take his time." He reached for the coil of line still on the dock, then sat down on the gunwale and got out his pocket knife. "Is it true he's bringing those women?"

Summer came back on deck. "He is," she said, taking one of the deck chairs. She watched idly as Joe deftly frayed the end of the line before weaving it back in the rope to form an eye.

He worked in silence for a moment. "That blonde's gonna be a pain," he remarked as he slipped his knife back in his pocket. He looked up, his face serious. "She ain't gonna like having you around."

Summer was startled by his perception. Surely she hadn't betrayed her chaotic feelings. How could she have? Joe hadn't been present. "What do you mean?" she asked slowly.

"You can see a lot from my kitchen window. That's why I like havin' my lunch there," he replied, seeming to change the subject.

Summer turned to gaze at his house, then back at him. She got the point. He had seen them together— yet, at that distance what could he have read? He couldn't know the impact Brandon's kiss had had on her.

"Tom's been gone a while now. I know that, but this ain't the man for you." His weathered face carried a tinge of red beneath his tan, but his faded eyes held hers steadily. "Not my business, I admit. In fact, you got every right to tell me to shut up."

The urge to do just that was strong. He made her

sound like a hot-pants widow and she didn't like it. For
five years she had poured her heart and soul into raising
Shannon and keeping Tom's business going. It hadn't
been easy. Heaven knows, it had been lonely. There
hadn't been time for men, and there were few around
willing to accept her as she was. The guys on the docks
did, but most of them were either married or too old.
The ones who weren't were only interested in a bounce
in the bunk. And that eliminated them. If she took a
man into her life, it wouldn't be a temporary arrangement. She knew herself well enough to know that she
wouldn't be able to handle it.

"I don't know what you think you saw, but I can
assure you Marshall is fully occupied with his friend."
The emphasis on the last word was unmistakable. "I
don't poach."

"Hell, girl, I wasn't talking about you," Joe all but
roared. "It's him. That man wants you, and if you
believe that little blond dolly is gonna hold him you're
nuts."

"Don't you think you're making a hurricane out of a
breeze?" she asked, beginning to get angry. "All we did
was discuss the arrangements for the trip." She purposely didn't mention the kiss.

"You didn't see him watching you from the end of the
dock. He was practically standing in my lap." Joe
registered her omission but made no references to it.

"That's enough." Her tone was sharper than any she
had ever used on her friend. Knowing him since she
was a child still didn't give him the right to come on like
a heavy-handed father. She was already too aware of
Brandon Marshall, and the last thing she needed was
Joe watching them like a hawk. "I don't want to hear
another word about the man." He started to speak.
"Not another sound. I mean it, Joe. I'm not a kid. I

don't need a keeper." The hurt in his eyes made her regret her sharpness. "I'm not in his girlfriend's league, believe me." Some of the hardness had left her voice.

"No, she's Little League, all right," he muttered under his breath before moving to the stern mooring cleat.

Summer pretended not to hear. One more comment would be too much. She wanted to forget the man's disturbing presence as quickly as possible. The thought of two weeks of his company under Joe's vigilance was enough to destroy what was left of her peace of mind.

"I'm heading for The Nest." She rose and stepped across to the dock. "See you in the morning."

Joe paused just long enough in removing the worn mooring line he was replacing to grunt in farewell.

As Summer strolled down the planking, she looked around her appreciatively, forcing Joe's warning from her mind. Tom would have been proud of his venture. Every mooring slip was rented, the bait shop was booming and the charter reservations were booked solid. They weren't rich but they were comfortable. Finally, The Nest was all theirs. The last installment to the bank a week ago was worth every bit of the effort it took to pay it off early. At this moment Tom's Rest and its owner were free and clear. If all went well, by the end of the season their account would be a healthy black.

Gussie came out of the shop as Summer went up the path. She waited while the older woman locked up.

"Where's Shannon?" Summer asked.

Gussie fell into step beside the younger girl. "I sent her on ahead. She needed a bath . . . badly." She chuckled. "That child! I told her to dust those storeroom shelves for me."

Summer stopped, letting Gussie precede her up the gangplank from the beach to the floating house's

37

entrance. "Let me guess. The dirt that came off the shelves ended up on her," she drawled in gentle humor.

"Got it in one," Gussie replied laughingly as she opened the front door.

The sound of Shannon's lilting off-key melody drifted from the bathroom, causing both women to exchange sympathetic glances.

"Whoever she marries better have a tin ear," Gussie remarked, shaking her head.

"If we live that long," Summer murmured as a particularly discordant screech reached them. "Shannon, are you dying?" she called, lifting her voice above the racket.

"Aw, Mom, it's my new song. Don't you just love it?" her daughter answered.

"We love it." She raised her eyebrows. "I bet Joe's glad the bait shop is between our two houses," she observed with a grin.

"Leave the child alone, Summer. After all, she takes after you."

"Why is it she's got my bad habits and Tom's good looks?"

"Lucky, I guess," her sister-in-law quipped. "Are you going to fix dinner or am I?"

"I'll do it," Summer decided, heading for her bedroom. "Let me get a shower first."

She opened the door of the room she had once shared with Tom. Pausing, she looked around. The aqua and white striped drapes muted the sun's rays, bathing the off-white walls in cool tones. The matching bedspread covered the huge, king-size bed, which seemed suddenly wasted on just her. The white wicker furniture she loved so was a feminine reminder of her manless state.

She pulled off her shirt with an angry movement. How could one male upset her equilibrium so much? She had never questioned her life-style before. She unsnapped her shorts and stepped out of them.

Clad in her flesh-tone briefs and bra, she padded to the matching aqua bathroom and turned on the shower taps. For a long moment she studied her reflection in the floor-length mirror. The image staring back at her seemed no different. Tall, thin as usual, she thought in silent self-mockery. And Joe believed the blonde would be jealous. Ha! The steam misted the glass, blurring her contours. She slipped out of her remaining clothes and stepped under the warm spray.

She must stop this now. She was no teenager to be bowled over by a handsome face and a sexy body. So she was attracted to him—who wouldn't be? But that's as far as it went. As far as she would *let* it go. By the time she left her room and headed for the upper deck, Summer was in control again. Brandon Marshall and his devastating appeal were firmly banished from her mind.

She entered the kitchen on bare feet, opened the refrigerator and took out the steaks for supper. As she passed the window over the sink she paused, glancing out across the inlet in appreciation. She loved her water home, she thought with a smile of pleasure as she began her dinner preparations. Long practice, first with her widower sea-captain father and later with Tom, made her work quickly and efficiently. Thinking about her husband brought his image to mind. The serious green eyes, the blond hair sprinkled with silver, the leanness that was curiously his own. She missed his quiet strength, the reassurance he gave the grief-stricken girl of eighteen ten years ago. It had been so natural then to turn to her father's closest friend for comfort and love. The fifteen years difference in their ages didn't seem to matter. Barely a month after her father's death, she married him—oddly enough with Joe's approval and Gussie's disapproval.

Summer slid the broiler pan into the oven without turning on the heat. She moved to the side counter to prepare the salad. Caught in visions of the past, she hardly noticed what she did.

Gussie's long ago words sounded in her ears as clearly as Shannon's singing had earlier. "Do you realize what you're doing, Summer? Tom is almost old enough to be your father. Surely you can see that? You're a beautiful girl. Give yourself time to adjust to Robert's death. Don't rush into this."

The young Summer's hurt was reflected in her eyes. "I thought you were my friend, Gussie. Don't you think I can make him happy?" she asked sadly.

"Yes," Gussie replied with something of a snap, "but can he make you happy? Does he make the world spin for you? Does he drive every thought from your head when he steps in the room? Does your body cry out for his touch?"

Summer stared at the older woman, moved almost to tears by her passionate questions. She couldn't answer because she could not lie to her. Gussie had been the only mother figure in her life for so long. Although she was almost fifty now, she had been young enough in spirit to guide Summer through countless adolescent crises.

The memory of Gussie's saddened face and her last whispered words brought a veil of tears to darken Summer's golden eyes. "You don't love him, child, not like a man should be loved by his woman."

The click of Gussie's light step on the spiral staircase made her wipe her eyes hurriedly with the back of her hand. It took an effort for Summer to force a smile to her lips as Gussie entered the second-floor kitchen.

"Shall I set the table?" Gussie asked, opening the linen drawer.

Summer nodded. "I guess so. It doesn't look like Shannon is going to do it."

"No chance. We run a poor second to cartoons," she agreed.

Gussie shook out the yellow linen and spread it over the round captain's table while Summer set the steaks to broil and started the French fries.

"What did you think of Brandon Marshall in the daylight?" her sister-in-law teased as she placed the white china with its yellow border on the table.

Summer's hand didn't tremble as she lifted the potatoes from the hot oil. "Sexy," she answered honestly.

"I'm glad you noticed. I was beginning to think you were going blind," she replied somewhat tartly.

Summer glanced up at that. "What are you getting at?" she asked, her gaze wary as she made no pretense of watching the food.

Gussie faced her squarely across the long bar that separated the eating area from the kitchen. "I mean you have nearly buried yourself alive since Tom died. Don't you think it's time you quit feeling guilty? Stopped trying to make up the disappointment you felt he had in you?"

Summer's face lost some of its color as her words sank in. "Is that what you believe I'm doing?"

The older woman nodded, her eyes compassionate. "Tom loved you and he accepted the love you had for him gratefully. It satisfied him the way it was; in your heart you know it did. Quit punishing yourself for the passion that was missing. Tom married you knowing that in many ways he was a stand-in for your father. He realized it and accepted it. You must, too." She paused, trying to decide whether to go on. Summer was no longer the child of her heart. She was a grown woman with needs, desires that deserved fulfillment. "It's time to start a new life for yourself. Put away the past, look into the future. Shannon needs a father, but most of all, you need a man. Someone to share the little things as well as the big. Someone to care for and to lean on."

Summer smiled slightly. "I think we've had this conversation before," she murmured.

"We did. Then perhaps I was wrong. You did make my brother happy. You were a good wife to him, but now it's your turn."

"You make it sound so easy. It's not. Times have changed. Women jump in and out of bed at the drop of a hat. Men even expect it, but that's not for me. I need more than that."

"Of course you do," Gussie agreed without hesitation. "Did I say you didn't?"

The pop of grease from the oven drew their attention for a moment.

"Blast!" Summer muttered, making a grab for the pot holder with one hand and the oven door with the other.

Although slightly crisp around the edges, the steaks were still edible. Gussie came behind the counter to peer at them as Summer turned them over.

"Do you mind if we stash this discussion until after I finish ruining this sirloin?" Summer asked when she slid the broiler pan back in the oven. "At the price I paid I think the least we can do is get it cooked decently."

"Aye, aye, Captain."

Summer glanced at her sister-in-law sharply, not missing the dry tone. She knew Gussie was by no means finished with her. Iron willed to the backbone, she never left a job half done. And it appeared that make-over-Summer was her current project.

Fortunately the older woman's common sense was almost as great as her determination. She left the younger woman alone during the meal that followed.

Summer knew the subject was far from closed. Gussie's words had dug deep into her past and her relationship with Tom, spotlighting feelings she had ignored at the time. Half of her listened to Shannon's chatter and made the appropriate responses. The other part of her mind examined her life.

Was she really unconsciously feeling guilty because her love for Tom had never risen beyond a gentle, comfortable affection? Was that why she found it easier not to date? Was she secretly afraid she would betray Tom and his love if she found a man who could move her to passion? Maybe she was frigid. She was twenty-eight. Surely by now if such a person existed, she would have met him.

She hardly noticed doing the dishes and seeing Shannon to bed. Her chaotic thoughts gave her no rest. Her steps lagged as she mounted the stairs to the upper deck. For once she was not looking forward to the quiet evening time they shared. She would have liked to plead tiredness, but she knew darned well her sister-in-law would see through the excuse. She took a deep breath and slid open the glass doors to the houseboat's terrace.

Gussie sat in her usual spot in the far corner away from the light spilling from the family room. Summer joined her silently, her feet making little sound on the chocolate-colored synthetic carpet. She sat down and propped them on the protective railing around the open deck.

"Gorgeous evening, isn't it?" Gussie remarked as she poured coffee from the pot on the table beside her into a second mug and handed it to Summer.

She sipped appreciatively, her eyes on the night-shrouded scene in front of her. "You wouldn't believe last night ever happened to see it now," she commented quietly.

The sky overhead was a black velvet canvas sprinkled with diamond stars. A breeze, carrying the tangy, clean scent of the ocean played softly through the pines and rippled the inky inlet channel with teasing fingers. Across the way the lighthouse made its rhythmic sweep, briefly showering the heavens with gold.

Instead of finding peace at the end of the day, Summer found she was oddly restless. She shifted irritably in her chair, calling herself all kinds of a fool to let Gussie's well-meant meddling disturb her.

"Something wrong, dear?" Gussie hadn't missed Summer's preoccupation at dinner and was secretly pleased that her words had not been wasted.

She loved this girl like she was her own. She had watched her grow up, had listened to her troubles and dried her tears. In her childless life Summer was the closest thing she had to a daughter. She wanted to see her happy, not half alive as she was now. So many times in the past few years she had ached to shake Summer out of her self-imposed role. Now she finally had the courage to speak, and she had no intention of losing her opportunity.

"Did you mean what you said?" Summer asked in a low voice, her face still turned to the water.

Gussie studied her profile. She couldn't tell much from her expression and even less from her tone of voice. "Which time?" she asked gently.

"That you think I'm locking myself away because of guilt?" She faced her relative, her eyes troubled.

Gussie shook her head. "Not really. There are many kinds of loving, just as there are many types of men. When my Jim died I was so sure there would never be another man for me I didn't look. Maybe I should have. I might have found him and had a family, something I have always missed." She paused, her gaze fixed on Summer's face. "I think of you as my daughter. Did you know that?" She reached to touch her hand for a second. "Don't hide from life. There just aren't that many days of it to use. Don't grow old regretting what you didn't try."

Summer caught the wrinkled fingers in hers. "You're not old, never to me. You're just right for an almost thirty-year-old daughter."

A film of tears sparkled in the pale blue eyes. Gussie's hand squeezed hers. "Now that's settled," she began with a determined smile. "What about this Marshall. That's some kind of man."

Summer released Gussie's hand with a jerk. "You can't be serious," she gasped. "I told you he brought his own entertainment. One well-stacked blonde."

"So?"

"So? So! Are you out of your tiny mind? You've seen his pictures in the paper often enough to know he's got a female in every city in the world," Summer answered heatedly.

"Hardly every city." Gussie replied mildly as she helped herself to more coffee. "What are you so steamed about, anyway? Don't tell me you've already considered it?"

"I did not . . ." she began indignantly.

Gussie's eyebrows raised at her vehemence. "Didn't you?" she murmured over the rim of her mug.

Blast! Summer could cheerfully have bitten her own tongue. Damn that man! She took a large swallow of her coffee, mentally counting to ten. After all her fine talk about putting him out of her mind.

"Okay, I'll admit he's what every woman probably dreams about. But not me. If I marry again—and that's a big if—it won't be to an international jet-setter, whatever his physical attraction."

"So you admit there is an attraction."

She nodded. "I do, but that's all there is or can be. I'll take him and his guests on the boat for two weeks, do my job, then wave goodbye. Finished. The end. He goes back to his world while I stay in mine." She drained her mug and set it on the table, suddenly tired of the subject. "I'm going in. Are you coming?" she asked as she rose to her feet.

"In a minute, dear. You go ahead, I'll lock up."

Summer stood unmoving for a moment. "I know you mean well, Gus, but I'll find my own way. I did listen, really." She searched the older woman's face in the darkness.

"I understand, child," she replied quietly. "Sweet dreams."

Summer's sleep was anything but pleasant. Brandon's face, vividly alive, haunted her dreams. He stood over her as she lay at his feet on a bare white-sand beach. His sea-colored eyes shone with the triumph of the chase, his bare chest gleamed a dark bronze in the moonlight. She was caught helpless by his stare. Her lungs gasped for air from her useless flight to escape capture.

"You're mine," his deep velvet voice whispered along her nerve endings, causing her eyes to widen with a primitive fear.

"No! no!" Summer groaned, to be jerked awake by

46

the sounds of her own low moans. She sat up in the darkness, her heart pounding in her breast. Her fingers clenched the aqua sheets in tension.

"Will you go away?" she begged in despair to the empty room. "I don't want you in my life or in my mind."

3

~~~~~~~~~~~~

Summer was too busy during the next two days to give much time to examining her conflicting feelings. If Brandon's disturbing face figured largely in her thoughts, she determinedly put it down to the preparations going on for his charter. Other than a phone call that Gussie placed to let him know she had confirmed hotel reservations at Treasure Cay, they had heard nothing from him.

As she lay awake in the predawn hours of Saturday, waiting for her alarm to go off, she tried to make some sense of her inner turmoil. In one way, Gussie was right; she did need something more in her life. If nothing else, her instantaneous reaction to Brandon showed her that. He triggered feelings she had never experienced before. But then he was the most personable, magnetic male she had ever met. She just wasn't entirely sure what she did want . . . yet. But she intended to find out.

The buzz of her bedside digital told her she had better get cracking. She flung back the aqua sheets and padded to the closet. Since the sky was already pale with the rising sun, she didn't bother with the lights. The aroma of fresh-brewed coffee told her Gussie was up and making breakfast. After pulling on her jeans and a pale blue tee-shirt, she gave her hair a quick brush. Finished, with all but the deck shoes she would put on just before she left, she picked up her windbreaker from the chair and headed upstairs to the kitchen. This morning she definitely needed her coffee.

"Good morning, Summer. How did you sleep?" Gussie asked cheerfully from in front of the stove. "Do you want one egg or two?"

"Fine, thank you, and two," she replied, answering both questions at once. She went over to the coffee pot, took a mug from the cabinet and filled it. Leaning one hip against the counter, she sipped the black liquid slowly, watching the older woman while she cooked.

"I hope I have remembered everything."

Surprised at the oddly unsure comment, Gussie glanced at her. If there was one thing Summer knew it was boats. She had grown up on and around them. Even the trip to the Bahamas was nothing out of the ordinary. She had lost count long ago of how many times Summer had been there.

"Something wrong?" She picked up their two plates and carried them to the table.

Summer laughed a little uncertainly. The last thing she wanted to do was explain her churning emotions. Gussie's matchmaking instincts were sure to surface. She didn't feel up to coping with any more of her home-grown philosophy. "Not really—nerves, maybe." She sat down and stared at the bacon and eggs on her plate. Suddenly she wasn't hungry anymore. Only the thought of Gussie's inevitable questions made her pick up her fork and take the first bite.

"You aren't worried about Shannon and me, are you?" Gussie persisted as she, too, began to eat.

Summer shook her head. "Most of our clients aren't

49

so famous. Maybe I'm overawed," she suggested in self-mockery. She mentally winced at the lame excuse. She was acting the coward for not admitting Brandon, the man, not his fame, bothered her.

"Pooh! You know what I think?"

"No, but I'm sure you're going to tell me."

Her pert answer brought a reproving look. "I think you don't want to spend fourteen days cooped up with that Joyce."

"Joyce . . . the blonde?" she asked in surprise. She nearly laughed out loud in relief at her answer.

Gussie nodded to emphasize her remark. Summer was reserved to the point of silence, and Gussie was more than a little miffed to have found out secondhand about Marshall's girlfriend. He had been so nice, too.

"Joe's been telling me what a mess she was the night you towed them in. What I can't figure out is why she's going if she hates boats so much."

Summer stared into her coffee cup like a fortune teller over her tea leaves. "She'd had a scare, Gus, that's all. If you could have seen how upset she was . . . Besides, I don't think the *Shalimar* was the attraction," she murmured before she drained the mug and set it down. She glanced at her watch. Thankfully, she didn't have time to linger any longer. She sensed Gussie gearing up to start on her again. "I must get going. They're due shortly."

Gussie followed her downstairs, waiting while she slipped on her shoes.

"I'll just pop in and say goodbye to Shannon," Summer said as she tied her laces.

Shannon's first floor room faced east, so the early morning sun filtered through the drapes, outlining the tiny figure in the ship's bunk. The soft yellow walls and pecan furniture were gay and feminine to suit its small mistress. The double-tiered glass shelf under the windows was empty of its usual occupants. Shannon had them all in bed with her.

Summer could barely distinguish her daughter's blond head among the various dolls keeping her company. She crossed over silently and knelt beside the bunk.

"Honey, I'm going now," she whispered softly. She waited patiently as the sandy lashes flickered and raised.

"'Bye, Mom." The tiny voice was drowsy, more asleep than awake.

Summer brushed her lips across her small forehead. "Be a good girl for auntie."

The curly head nodded. "You too, Mom," she mumbled before drifting off again.

Gussie was still waiting in the hall when she closed Shannon's door.

"Joe just collected the cooler." She handed Summer her windbreaker, watching while she slipped into it. "Now, I've got the number for the Treasure Cay Hotel. I think that's it."

Summer grinned. "Don't get into your boss-lady role yet. I haven't even left the dock."

Gussie's answering chuckle instantly banished her serious expression. "You know the saying: Give a woman a little power . . ."

She held up her hand in mock surrender. "I'm going, I'm going." She was halfway down the gangplank to the beach when Gussie called from the door. She was halfway down the gangplank to the beach when Gussie called from the door.

"Take care, Captain."

Summer waved without turning around. For a fleeting instant she felt the prickle of tears in her eyes. Odd, how she and Gussie had taken to using the same ritual of saying goodbye as she and Tom once had. The gestures, the little jokes, all indications of deep caring.

While it carried a special meaning for her and her sister-in-law, it lacked the overlay of passion present between a man and his wife facing a separation. Had she really missed so much? She again felt irritated at Gussie for waking her to the possibilities. She was angry at herself, too. This new questioning made her vulnerable and she didn't like it. With the physical attraction she felt for Brandon Marshall, she didn't need that, too. His arrival had destroyed the even pace of her existence. Joe watched her like a guard dog, Gussie had forced her to examine her feelings and she . . . Well, she just had to see to it that Brandon Marshall stayed where he belonged—both figuratively and literally, she decided with single-minded determination. He was a client, nothing more, nothing less. She would keep it that way. Her brisk, free-swinging stride down the dock to the *Sea Mist's* berth punctuated her resolution. Long years of self-discipline pushed Brandon's attraction into the far recesses of her mind, allowing her to concentrate on the job at hand.

Summer automatically glanced at the sky, noting the golden-pink flush staining the eastern horizon. The breeze from the ocean was gentle, carrying the subtle fragrance of the mating of the land and the sea. The dawn held the promise of a beautiful day.

Joe stood at the stern of the boat, finishing his last-minute check. He looked up at her soft-footed approach. "Ain't they here yet?" he greeted her sourly.

Accustomed to his early morning grouchiness, she ignored his tone. She glanced over her shoulder, down the empty dock and the sparsely filled parking area under the trees. Recognizing the cars of the regulars, she shook her head. "Not that I can see." She stepped across the gunwale to the deck.

Joe checked the boldfaced watch on his wrist. "I'll

bet that blonde didn't want to get up," he observed under his breath. "They should be here by now."

Summer studied her mate worriedly. "Just what did Joyce say to you, anyway? You never did tell me."

He glared at her. "Ain't what she said so much as how she acted. High-bred lady, dahling." He drawled the last word out to a sneer. "Might not be rich and born in Boston, but I ain't no peasant, either."

"Remember, she's a customer just like her boyfriend." The faint twist of pain at her own description caught her unaware. She sternly ignored it.

"I remember, all right." He looked toward the parking lot as a cream LTD pulled to a stop. "It looks like they're here . . . finally."

Summer turned to greet her passengers, her expression professional with the right touch of friendliness. Her eyes slid over the two women as they came down the dock, taking in the expensive designer jeans, deck shoes and matching tops, a deep pink for Joyce and a soft yellow for the dark-haired Amy. Behind them both men carried two large suitcases each, leaving the girls to bring a smaller case apiece.

"Here, let me take that," Summer offered, extending a hand to Amy.

"Thank you anyway, but no," she replied with a cheerful grin. She threw an impish look over her shoulder at her husband. "Chuck swore I had to do everything for myself if I came along."

Summer tried to suppress her amusement at Chuck's expression. "All right, then be careful stepping over," she cautioned, keeping a wary eye on the younger woman. She turned to offer to help Joyce aboard.

"You may have mine." Joyce handed her burden over without being asked. Although her voice was pleasant, there was no mistaking the command.

Summer caught Chuck's eye as the other woman stepped carefully across. There was a decided twitch to his lips as he looked down at the dock. Summer hadn't missed the faint wink he gave her.

No wonder Joe was set against having that woman aboard. Obviously, her abruptness the night of the rescue wasn't due solely to fear and shock. Thank heavens Chuck and his wife were along. At least they were friendly. Behind her she could hear Amy exclaiming over the vee-bunks under the bow. She must have followed Joe forward when he stowed their luggage. Even Joe's grunts to her questions didn't impair her enthusiasm.

Brandon was the last to come across, his long legs making short work of the distance between the *Sea Mist's* gunwale and the dock.

"Is that all your gear?" Summer asked in a business-like tone, carefully concealing the reaction she felt to his presence.

Like the rest of them, he wore denims, faded a soft blue by repeated washings. They were belted low on his hips, fitting his lean body without a crease. The open-neck cream knit shirt revealed an expanse of bronzed chest and muscled arms. He looked crisp, cool and vibrantly male.

"We're traveling light," he agreed, his voice reaching out to stroke her nerve endings, sending a chill up her spine.

Briefly Summer met his eyes, keeping her own expression calm. His impersonal but friendly gaze reassured her. The knowing awareness of their last meeting was absent. There was no reminder of the kiss they had shared. She felt the tension in her body slowly unwind and smiled.

"Want me to take those?" Joe asked, coming up behind them.

Brandon handed over his two cases. They grouped together around Summer. Joyce laid a possessive hand on Brandon's arm, drawing his attention. "I thought you said there was a cabin where I could lie down?" she asked on a faintly plaintive note.

A flicker of annoyance crossed Brandon's face. "There is, Joyce, under the bow. This is a working boat, so don't expect it to be what you're accustomed to," he stated flatly.

Summer watched as the blonde glanced around the wide uncluttered deck, then at the small under-roof cockpit area with its foldable eating table and padded bench. The two single chairs facing forward were comfortable but hardly plush. Under the bow there were bunks with ample room to stretch out but definitely nothing like the staterooms aboard the *Shalimar*.

The *Sea Mist* was a fishing boat, and she looked the part. From the top of her tuna tower rising above the flybridge to her blue waterline she was a sturdy craft, well-fitted and depended on to perform her job.

Summer felt no need to apologize for her and was pleased Brandon hadn't done so, either. "Since everything's on board, we can get underway," she announced. She sat down on the edge of the boat, one knee crooked for comfort, to explain what happened next. This was mostly for the girls' benefit, although from what she could see of Chuck's avid expression, it was new to him also.

"It's an easy run to Treasure Cay from here and we'll arrive sometime after noon. There's not much to see on the crossing except open water, and we won't be slowing to fish unless we spot something especially promising." She paused for a second as Joe joined the group. "You can sunbathe if you like or sleep. The bunks are made up. Joe is the first mate, and he'll help with the tackle, boating the fish and so forth. If you have any questions, he'll be able to help. Usually I'm up there." She gestured to the small platform above the cabin, covered by a canvas top. "Lunch will be about twelve unless you would prefer something sooner." She glanced questioningly at Brandon.

"No, that's fine."

She nodded. "There are beer and soft drinks in the fridge, also coffee and donuts. That's about it, I think." She stood up. "Is there anything I've left out?" She glanced around the listening group.

Seeing no one had any questions, she headed for the small aluminium foot grids leading to the flybridge, leaving a babble of voices behind.

"Oh, Chuck, this is going to be fun," Amy enthused. "I'm glad you talked me into coming. Just imagine fourteen days without children, telephones and business, not to mention the cold we left behind. I can't believe how warm it is. Here, let's sit in these chairs." She tucked her arm into her husband's with a smile.

Joe was busy with the mooring lines, leaving Brandon and Joyce standing where Summer had left them.

"I think I'll lie down," Joyce purred softly with a provocative sweep of her lashes. The open construction of the boat gave little privacy. Other than the small cabin in the bow section, there was nowhere else to go. The close quarters eliminated any possibility for intimacy.

Brandon eyed her, not missing the invitation in her look. "That's a good idea," he agreed, ignoring her invitation. "As the captain said, there won't be much to see anyway."

Joyce's eyes narrowed slightly at his easy dismissal. "I'd hoped you would join me."

He shook his head, his gaze going to the flybridge.

Joyce followed his glance, a speculative gleam entering her eyes. "She's a widow, isn't she?" she asked with seemingly idle curiosity.

"Yes, she is," Brandon agreed without looking back at her. Joyce could tell little from his expression. She had tried her damnedest to get him to propose. She had been so certain she would succeed on this trip. But circumstances had blocked her at every turn. First the Bartos had appeared to shatter the cosy twosome trip she had planned when she invited herself along on this trip. Then the *Shalimar's* disaster had made him unapproachable. Not to mention her occasional bouts of seasickness and the terror she felt when the storm had nearly sunk them all.

Now they were cooped up on a fishing boat with a woman captain—a beautiful woman at that, she admitted fairly. She wasn't especially fond of her own sex, but she was honest, at least with herself. She felt her temper rise, but she fought it down. She knew anger would gain her nothing. Brandon was tough. No woman, not even she, had a chance of demanding anything from him and getting it. Softness was the ticket.

"You'll call me for lunch?" she asked quietly, gaining his attention again.

Brandon saw the disappointed look on her face at his refusal. "Sure. Afterwards you can show off that new bikini you bought. I'm sure the captain won't mind if you sunbathe on the stern," he offered with a slight smile.

Joyce's eyes gleamed with triumph beneath their screen of lashes as she turned away. Brandon watched her for a moment as she walked slowly toward the cabin before he turned in his friends' direction.

"Look at that," Amy cried, pointing to three pelicans making dive-bomb swoops at the schooling mullet near the mouth of the inlet. "You would never believe such an ugly bird could be so beautiful in flight."

"He's built for his needs," Brandon said with a grin. Amy looked over her shoulder, her eyes dancing with excitement.

"She acts about ten, doesn't she?" Chuck teased and ruffled her dark brown curls affectionately.

"She does," Brandon agreed. "Joyce is lying down for a while, so I think I'll see if it's all right to visit the captain."

"Sure it is," Joe answered, catching the question as he stopped beside him. "Careful, though; don't wanna fish you out of the water." He turned to the other couple. "You two like anything to drink? Coffee?"

Brandon moved away before either of them answered. He mounted the slender rung extending up the outside of the cabin, feeling the wind pulling at his clothes. He paused when his waist was level with the deck of the flybridge. "May I come up? Joe said he thought it would be okay."

Summer started at the sound of his voice. "Come ahead, there's room." She moved over slightly, then braced her legs again against the motion of the boat. She didn't speak until Brandon stood beside her. "Everybody settled?" she asked as she checked the compass in front of her and adjusted her heading slightly.

"Amy is having the time of her life and Chuck is enjoying watching her."

"And Miss Fielding?" she prompted, curious about the blonde.

"She's sleeping," he answered flatly and then paused for a second before continuing in an altered tone. "I owe you an explanation."

Summer glanced at him, surprised. "What for?"

"Joyce isn't very accustomed to boats. Don't let her comments bother you."

He didn't look at her as he spoke but stared straight ahead. Summer studied his profile, the brown hair ruffled by the wind. She felt his discomfort at having to make excuses for his girlfriend.

She shrugged. "Forget it. I've heard a lot worse, believe me."

She sat on the bench seat, keeping one hand on the wheel. The glare of the sun reflecting from the water made her reach for her sunglasses lying on the console. The relief from the bright glare was instantaneous.

After a moment Brandon joined her on the seat, stretching his legs in front of him. "She runs nice," he commented, referring to the boat. "How long have you had her?"

"About six years. Tom bought her the year before he died."

"Was he a captain, too?" he asked curiously, watching the competent way she handled the controls.

Summer's smile flickered briefly. "Yes. He got the *Sea Mist* the day I passed my captain's exam. We both were drenched in champagne to christen our maiden voyage." Memories of the dock party, culminating in her breaking a bottle over the *Sea Mist's* bow and Tom showering her with another, flooded her mind.

"What was he like?" Brandon questioned. He was surprised at the urge he felt to know about the man she had married—the man who had fathered her child.

Caught in a tangle of time-dimmed images, Summer forgot for a moment the identity of her listener. She was at home here on the open sea, the wind brushing her hair, the limitless sky ahead. This was the life she loved and Tom had been a part of it. "He was gentle, comfortable to be with. Dependable in an emergency and caring. He loved the water. He was a good father to Shannon." Her voice trailed away.

Brandon noted the absence of her feelings. "What about as a husband?" he prompted quietly.

Summer came back to the present with a start, turning to stare at him. Suddenly she was glad of the protective mirrored lenses to hide her shock at how much she had revealed. What was it about this man that made her forget her usual reserve?

"He was a good husband," she responded coolly, withdrawing once more. "He took care of me while he lived and he left me with a livelihood to provide for both Shannon and me when he died."

Brandon's face showed only impersonal interest as he met her gaze. He felt her mental retreat and made a good guess at its cause. He wondered what feelings those golden eyes held behind their protective silver screens. Did she realize how incomplete her relationship sounded? Where was the passion? The fire? Caring was hardly a substitute. Not for a woman like her. She needed more. He knew it, but did she?

"So then you became the captain of the *Sea Mist*," he observed, changing the subject slightly. He wanted to keep her talking to find out more about her. What she thought. What she felt. He couldn't remember ever having such a deep interest in a woman before.

There was a touch of defensive anger in her reply. "I did."

Brandon had the impression of a golden cat who had been stroked the wrong way. "I wasn't being patronizing," he explained, verbally smoothing the tawny fur back in place. "I really wanted to know."

Summer relaxed, her temper fading. She ran her free hand through her sun-streaked curls. "I'm afraid I always expect the worst from outsiders. It took me a long time to be accepted, and even now there are still a few diehards. I guess there always will be."

Brandon had to grin at her disgusted tone. "I can't say I blame them. Haven't you looked in the mirror?"

"What's that got to do with it?" She was honestly puzzled and it showed. She knew she was attractive, but she didn't realize how beautiful she was. Nor did she recognize the almost untamed quality of her appeal to the male sex. The two men in her life, Tom and her father, had paid little attention to her startling looks. Between her strict no-nonsense attitude with her charters and Joe's watchful presence, she had been spared most of the passes that would have come her way in other circumstances.

He shook his head wonderingly. In his world women knew their own beauty and more often than not exploited it. He found himself silenced by her total lack of awareness.

"This is Tango-Adam-Tango 9559 calling vessel *Sea Mist*. How about you, Summer girl?" The bell-clear voice on the VHF radio split the quiet.

Summer picked up the mike, pressing the transmit button as she did. "This is Tango-George-Sam 3873. Hi, Billy. I thought it was you," she answered with a smile in her voice. She held the *Sea Mist* steady on course even though her eyes were trained on the distinctive green hull of the *Sea Gull* a half mile ahead off the port side. "Looks like you've got a full load."

Brandon followed her gaze. The wide-bottom drift boat was covered with zealous anglers standing elbow to elbow around its gunwales and stern.

"Sure do. Hear you got a run yourself. Wanna trade places? I've got one lady on the tail who's tangled her line with the two men on either side of her at least three times. Eddie's baited hooks until he threatened to quit and it's only nine o'clock." The voice gave an artistic groan. "The Bahamas . . . sun-white beaches . . . Let's get away from it all. Pick me up and we'll ditch your charter and have some fun."

Summer laughed as she pictured herself next to Billy's five-foot-six-inch frame. In her bare feet she was at least two inches taller. Besides, he was fifty if he was a day.

"No go, my friend. You'll have to find some other willing woman to take you away from it all," she teased back. She felt Brandon's attention. She glanced at him out of the corner of her eye, noting his open curiosity.

"Well, I tried," Billy replied in mock resignation. "Have a good trip anyway." He signed off.

Summer replaced the mike. "You look as though you disapprove," she remarked.

Brandon pulled himself up short, surprised that he did. He hadn't liked the easy familiarity between Summer and the unknown Billy. How had that happened? He barely knew this woman. He had no valid reason to object to anyone she associated with.

"I don't have any right to judge. What you do is your own affair," he murmured, speaking his thoughts aloud. He rose to his feet, the breeze whipping at his hair now that he no longer sat protected by the windshield. "I'll go down and see how the others are doing."

Summer watched him leave with puzzled eyes. It was almost as though he were jealous. But that was crazy. They hardly knew each other, she argued, unknowingly echoing Brandon's own thoughts.

4

It was early afternoon by the time Summer sighted the verdant cluster of islands known as the Abacos. They were the easternmost chain of the Little Bahama Bank. Comprising approximately 650 square miles, the group boasted a number of small cays, many uninhabited. Some, like Walker's Cay and their own destination, Treasure Cay, were known in the angling world for their excellent fishing.

Summer stood up, stretching the stiffness from her muscles. Except for a short break for lunch when Joe took over, she had piloted the *Sea Mist* the entire 170-odd miles. She eased the throttle back, keeping one eye on the depth recorder and the other on the approaching coastline. Ahead stretched the small white-sanded tufts of land that guarded the circular bay of Treasure Cay. The sea changed quickly from the indigo blue of deep water to a sparkling green. She guided her craft expertly through the potentially dangerous shallows to the deeper channel beyond. The docks of the hotel were dead ahead. As they got closer, Summer saw the customs official waiting for them at the dockmaster's office. She brought the engines to idle speed as she edged her craft carefully between the mooring pilings. The *Sea Mist* nudged the wharf gently as it came to rest.

Below, she heard Joe warn everyone to stay on board for the customs inspection.

Amy's voice floated up. "Have you ever seen such colors? Just look at those flowers!"

Summer smiled to herself at Amy's continued enthusiasm and descended the grids to the deck. After sharing lunch with her four passengers, she had learned more about them. While Joyce had remained distant, Amy had more than made up for her attitude. Lively and full of questions, she had had them all laughing. Even the sophisticated blonde managed an occasional smile, although Summer suspected her limited participation was more for Brandon's benefit than for any other reason. It wasn't hard to see he was pleased with her change. She wondered again what made him select such a woman to take on this type of trip.

"Afternoon, Captain." The white-clad Bahamian customs officer greeted her. While his smile was wide and friendly, his appearance matched the cool precision of his British accent.

"Charles," Summer answered, handing over her papers for his scrutiny. Over her previous visits they had progressed to first names. "We should be here about fourteen days. Heard the fishing is better than usual."

The dark-skinned man made two checks on the papers attached to his clipboard before he looked up. "Your timing is excellent," he agreed, returning her credentials. He glanced at Brandon and his party as they sat at the *Sea Mist's* stern. "These all your passengers?"

Summer quickly introduced Brandon. As usual Charles' inspection was thorough but quick. In no time at all Joe was back from the dockmaster's office with their mooring assignment, announcing happily they'd been given a low number, placing them in the line of slips nearest the hotel and shore.

Summer eased the *Sea Mist* stern-first into her berth. At the bow Joe snubbed off the mooring lines while Brandon and Chuck secured the rear.

"You make it look so easy," Amy observed from her seat beside Summer. Since lunch she had become Summer's shadow. While Joyce had stripped to a brief electric-blue bikini and sunbathed on the deck, Amy had plied Summer with questions. Born in the Middle West, she had no experience at all with boats, so many of her queries were of the kindergarten variety. Summer didn't mind. She enjoyed the open manners of the brunette, especially when they had eventually got around to discussing their children.

"How do you get it to stop where you want it when there aren't any brakes?"

Summer grinned and pointed to the two white ropes extending to the huge gray pilings in front of the boat's bow. "See those? If I don't cut the power back to neutral soon enough for the *Mist* to drift to a stop, I would run out of line. They're my brakes. It's only a matter of timing and practice," she explained with a dismissing shrug as she killed the engines.

"I wish I could do something really well," Amy murmured with a sigh.

"Like what?"

"I don't know. I—"

"Are you finally going to break out of your house-wifey image?" Joyce questioned with amusement as she emerged from the cabinway between them. She stood up and leaned back casually against the windshield. "If you worked, think about all those cute little things the twins do that you would miss."

Summer was surprised to see the haughty look Amy

65

shot at the other girl. And then she stared her up and down once. Too often in the past she'd been subjected to Joyce's blunt comments about childbearing and homemaking. Just because she hadn't lifted a finger to do anything more than jet around the world several times, she felt everyone else's life was dull. "At least I'm useful to someone," Amy commented meaningfully, one eyebrow raised. She turned her swivel chair so that her shoulder was to the blonde, effectively ignoring her presence.

She returned to their interrupted conversation without a blink. "I enjoy my life, but I don't want the boys to grow up believing a woman is only good in the home. It's not a very realistic attitude. Besides, since Chuck got this last promotion he hired a full-time housekeeper, and now I have very little to keep me busy when Charlie and Chad are in school."

"If you two are going to talk kids, I think I'll help the men," Joyce announced abruptly, her cheeks stained red by temper and Amy's snub. She stalked by them to the stern, leaving the two women staring at each other.

"I wonder why Brand brought her along?" Amy mumbled softly.

Summer got to her feet, her eyes following the blonde's approach to Brandon's kneeling figure. She saw the scarlet-tipped hand trail suggestively up his smooth muscled back to rest on his shoulder as he bent over the stern, securing the mooring line to the cleat.

"He doesn't appear to feel she's out of place," she offered, nodding her head significantly in their direction. She stopped herself just in time from remarking on their closeness after lunch when Joyce had stretched out on her chaise to sunbathe, her body glistening with tanning oil. Brandon hadn't left her side then, and she had been all smiles and provocative glances.

"All secure, Summer." Joe stepped down from the

gunwale to the deck with a muted thump. "I'll see to the bags for you if ya'll wanna register," he offered as Brandon, with Joyce clinging like a limpet to his side, and Chuck came over to join them.

"Sounds good to me," Brandon agreed, glancing at his friend.

"The first thing I want to do is head for the pool. How about you, Amy?"

Amy picked up the floppy brimmed hat she had unearthed just after lunch and jammed it on her head. "Lead on, husband. I'm hot enough to settle for a bathtub if I had to."

"What about you?" Brandon asked Summer.

"I have a few things to see to, then I'll check myself in."

After Joe and her passengers disappeared up the path to the main building, Summer went below to exchange the chart she had used on the trip over for the ones she needed for the next day. By the time she finished collecting her bag and carrying it and the charts topside, Joe had returned.

"I'm off now." She heaved the duffel onto the dock. "After I shower, I think I'll stop by Salty's and pick up the latest fishing news."

"Good idea. I'll probably get over there after a bit when I finish cleanin' up. What time we leavin' in the mornin'?"

Summer paused for a split second, considering. "Daybreak, unless I tell you otherwise," she decided finally.

As she made her way up the stone-paved path to the hotel's main buildings, she mentally kicked herself for not asking Brandon when he wanted to start. She had looked forward to a few hours respite from watching him and his girlfriend. She had tried telling herself she was overreacting to Joyce's attitude, but it hadn't done any good. She needed some time by herself to get her perspective back. With the four of them lodged on the far side of the complex in one of the ocean townhouses away from her room in the main hotel, she would have the privacy she wanted.

She saw, without really noticing, the luxurious tropical *House and Garden*-type plantings along the gently curving trail. The exotic mixed fragrance of blooming hibiscus, oleander and ixora carried on the tangy salt air was at odds with her agitation. Despite herself, she found the lovely scene soothing. She would just phone Mr. Brandon Marshall if he wasn't at the pool and get the departure time, she decided. At least she didn't need to go to see him. Satisfied with her solution to the most immediate problem, her steps quickened as muted sounds of laughter and splashing came from around the next bend. The path ended at the outer terrace of a huge free-form pool surrounded by gay yellow-and-white-striped deck chairs. She skirted the crowded loungers, carefully scanning the bronze bodies for Brandon's distinctive figure. He wasn't in the water or seated at the outdoor bar at the far end of the patio.

She removed her sunglasses as she stepped into the reception area of the main building. The dim coolness was a relief from the hours of blinding glare on the open water. She paused for a moment and glanced around the casual island-style foyer. Treasure Cay was one of her favorite hotels. The bamboo and rattan decor coupled with the lush greenery of potted plants presented a beautiful and relaxed atmosphere to arriving guests. Even the unusual mustard yellow of the hotel's exterior seemed to blend in perfectly with the cay's landscape.

As Summer walked across to the registration desk, she drew more than one interested male stare—a fact she was unaware of. Her immediate concern was the possibility of a cool shower followed by a tall, icy drink. Then she would tackle phoning Brandon. The receptionist's gentle smile was another example of the Bahamian charm as she handed Summer her room key.

An hour later Summer left her room and headed once again in the direction of the pool. After telephoning Brandon's townhouse twice, she decided her best chance of catching him was to swing by the patio area. She spotted Joyce's bikini-clad shape almost at once, stretched provocatively on the far side of the pool. It took a moment longer to pick out the sleek dark heads of the other three as they lazed in the water near her reclining figure.

Amy looked up and saw her. "Hi, come on over," she called with a gay wave. She waited until Summer got closer. "You should have joined us."

Brandon eyed her trim figure with unconcealed interest. His eyes started at the slender leather-sandaled feet, traveling up the crisp, white, sailor-cut jeans and blue-striped knit top. His gaze lingered for a moment on the shadowed valley visible at the base of the deep vee-neck before finally settling on the tawny eyes. His lips curved in a slow smile at the dawning anger in the honeyed depths.

"I think it is we who should have joined our captain," he murmured audaciously.

Joyce looked from Brandon's teasing expression to Summer's purposely blank features, not liking the intrusion. "I thought you said you had work to do?" she observed with studied innocence.

Summer ignored her thinly veiled sarcasm, concentrating her attention on Brandon's face. "I forgot to find out when ya'll wanted to start in the morning." Her slow southern drawl was a definite improvement over Joyce's more nasal tone.

"I hope we can start later this time," Joyce pleaded from her carefully seductive position.

Brandon heaved himself over the pool edge in one swift, powerful motion. "Hand me a towel, Joyce," he directed.

Despite herself Summer found her eyes drawn to his magnificent body, the water running in rivulets over the smooth bronze skin. She had the strongest urge to slip her hands over those taut muscles and feel the crispness of the dark brown pelt across the wall of his chest.

Silent until now, Chuck entered the discussion. "I, for one, would rather go early. At least it's cooler then." He pulled himself out of the water and leaned over to give Amy a hand.

Summer thankfully turned her attention to the other couple as Amy added her voice to the argument. "Me, too." She accepted the towel her husband tossed her and patted her arms dry. "I'm slightly pink now as it is. I don't want to start my vacation with a sunburn."

Chuck glanced at her face and arms. "Amy! Why didn't you say something!" he exploded. "Of all the feather-headed stunts. You should be in the shade, not in this pool. You know how you burn."

"I don't believe this," Joyce murmured in disgust as she flopped back in her lounger and picked up the fashion magazine from the table at her side. "When you decide what we're going to do, let me know."

Summer looked from one face to another, ending with Brandon. She wished she had never bothered to set foot outside her room if this was the result of a simple question. Her thoughts showed clearly in her eyes, and Brandon's stare was alight with wicked amusement. Suddenly she found her exasperation melting as the humor of the situation struck her. She started to grin, triggering an answering response in the man watching. Her glance flickered to Amy and Chuck, who were squared off like two fighting cocks ready to do battle, then to Joyce's blonde head buried in her book, obviously ignoring them all.

Brandon draped the towel around his neck and moved to her side. He leaned down slightly until his lips were close to her ear. "Why don't we leave them to it," he whispered conspiratorially before cupping his hand under her elbow and drawing her a few steps to a nearby umbrella table. "I don't know about you, but I could do with a drink."

Summer sat down for the first time, feeling truly relaxed in his presence. "Sounds good."

He beckoned to a passing waiter and requested island coolers, a local nonalcoholic favorite made of various fruit juices served in a tall frosted glass.

"I hope you ordered me one of those," Joyce said. She looked up, proving she wasn't as divorced from her surroundings as she pretended. Rising, she made a production of sliding her narrow feet into her high-heeled sandals. Every movement, every gesture was designed to draw the male eye.

Summer found herself watching Brandon's reaction. She wasn't proud of the pleasure she felt at his cynically amused appraisal. It was becoming more difficult by the moment to remain in his presence. She couldn't let herself succumb to his charms. She had Shannon to think about if not her own self-respect. While she suspected part of Brandon's attraction for Joyce was his money and position, she knew the girl cared for him—possibly loved him. The hungry look in her eyes, her possessive behavior when another woman was around all shouted it. What would happen if he turned

71

his attention to her? Could she withstand the siege or would she surrender to the increasing desire firing her blood? The next fourteen days couldn't be over fast enough, she thought, as Joyce sank gracefully into the deck chair on Brandon's left and slid her arm through his.

Aquamarine eyes met Summer's stare, darkening at her expressionless face. Behind her golden shutters, Summer saw his mind probing the sudden change in her mood.

"I tell you I'm all right," Amy exclaimed, dropping into the empty seat beside Summer.

Summer turned to face her, breaking loose from Brandon's visual hold.

The waiter arrived with their drinks, silencing Chuck's retaliation. The moment Chuck had finished ordering the same for himself and his wife, Brandon spoke.

"Chuck's right, you know, Amy. It isn't smart to underestimate the sun even at this time of year." He surveyed his friend's triumphant look with a smile. "She's right too, old man. She's not really that red."

Amy giggled at her husband's deflated expression. "If I had my drink, I would toast the peacemaker," she teased with a mischievous glance in Brandon's direction.

Summer, unfortunately for her, had just taken a sip of her cooler. One look from under her lashes at Brand's stunned expression over Amy's comment had Summer hurriedly swallowing before she choked. It had to be a new role for Brandon—marital referee.

Tired of being left out of the conversation, Joyce voiced her opinion, totally ignoring the banter going on around her. She showed her lack of a sense of humor. "I vote for ten o'clock, at least. After all, we won't want to miss the midnight show in the lounge. The girl at the desk said it was quite something."

"What are you talking about?" Amy asked, glancing first at Joyce, then Brandon.

"Why, the floor show, of course," she answered, surprised. "Brandon promised to show me the sights and take me dancing." She leaned her smooth golden head against his bare shoulder.

He gazed down at her. "I did promise you dancing, but I don't remember saying it would be the night we arrived." He reached for his glass, forcing Joyce to release his arm. "Why don't we leave about eight—that should satisfy everyone," he suggested.

"That's fine with us," Chuck agreed after a questioning look at his wife. He picked up her hand. "I don't mind a little pink, but I draw the line at red."

"It's settled, then."

"But what about my dancing, darling? You promised." Joyce's little-girl pout was a masterpiece of acting.

Brandon wasn't fooled by her machinations. The vision of Summer's freshly scrubbed beauty, her slow, melodic speech and her spontaneous humor left him oddly dissatisfied with Joyce. Always in the past he had sought and found the lacquered sophisticate, the woman who knew the score. One who wanted neither commitments nor marriage. Although Joyce had made it clear recently she wanted more, he knew her heart was not really involved.

"Well?" she prompted when he didn't answer immediately.

"All right. After dinner I'll take you to the lounge." He sighed, tossing off the rest of his drink. He glanced at Chuck. "Do you two want to come?"

"I think not, not dancing, anyway. Supper sounds fine."

"What about you, Summer?" Amy asked. "You've probably made this trip often enough not to be tired."

"I still feel the effects, believe me," she replied. "I'm for an early night, too. And I want to call Shannon."

"Are you dressing for dinner?"

"No, I'm going to put my feet up and let room service do the work," she replied, rising.

Amy's expression reflected her puzzlement. "Aren't you joining us?" She glanced at Brandon for enlightenment.

He wasn't quite fast enough to cover his momentary blank look. Summer saw the pink creep into Amy's cheeks as she realized her blunder. Charter captains were not normally invited to dinner with the clients.

"Now Amy, how am I going to maintain a tight ship if I fraternize with the passengers? I must keep my tough old-salt image, you know," Summer teased with a grin.

Amy's flush subsided, but she was still unconvinced. "I don't see why you can't have dinner with us," she insisted stubbornly.

"Because you don't eat with your chauffeur," Joyce commented bluntly, smiling as if to take the sting from her words.

Summer's eyes blazed as she surveyed Joyce's challenging stare. Her hand wrapped around her ice-filled glass, and for an instant she debated dumping it on her. But the image of Joyce's shrieking reaction surprisingly cooled her temper. Her lips twitched as she visualized the faces of her friends.

"You ought to watch your sense of humor," Brandon warned quietly, his eyes fastened on his girlfriend's face. "Not everyone appreciates it." He turned to Summer, ignoring Joyce's shrug of unconcern. "We'll meet you in the lobby at seven-thirty."

Summer opened her mouth to voice her refusal, then closed it. His silent command to say, *Yes, thank you* was crystal clear and undeniable.

"I'll be there," she murmured, glancing toward the others in an effort to appear normal. Neither Amy nor her husband showed any awareness of the byplay that had gone on between Summer and Brandon.

A minute later, breathing a sigh of relief, she passed out of sight of their table and made her way to the waterfront and Salty's place. Until that second, she had not realized how tense she was. No matter how often she tried to tell herself differently, she still was unable to contain her response to Brandon's presence. For the first time in her life, she found she couldn't escape her thoughts. Her mind said there wasn't and never could be any future with Brandon Marshall, but her treacherous senses were deaf to its warnings.

By the time Summer opened her hotel room door later that evening, she was ready for bed. She had the beginnings of an uncharacteristic headache. It had started with her own body's traitorous reactions to Brandon. Sitting next to him, listening to his velvet voice, had triggered vivid memories of his lips on hers. It was as though he were the only man in the room. No matter how much she tried to suppress her clamoring senses, she had found her eyes drawn to the curve of his mouth. It was foolish—suicidal even—to fantasize a relationship between them.

Joyce's flagrantly sexy behavior had been the final straw to her throbbing head. Even Chuck and Amy's presence didn't cool the blonde's ardor. What was worse, Brandon did nothing to curb her blatant display. While he had been scrupulously polite, his mind was clearly fixed on something else. And it didn't take much guesswork on her part to figure out the cause, Summer thought in disgust. Who could help but notice when a voluptuous body was draped all over you—a half-clothed one at that. Personally, she wouldn't have touched that hot-pink halter dress on a bet. A bikini covered twice as much.

Summer eased out of her own emerald-green sheath and regarded it ruefully. If she had wanted to compete with Joyce for Brandon's attention, she wouldn't have stood a chance. The scooped-out neck of the delicate frond-patterned cotton was puritanically modest when compared to the throat-to-waist slash of the other girl's outfit, nor did the flared skirt, which molded her hips so smoothly, appear special against daring thigh slits.

As she lay awake in the darkness waiting for sleep to extinguish her body's restless dissatisfaction with her empty bed, she wondered if Brandon had succumbed to Joyce's enticing luring.

Summer was sure she had her answer when a smiling Joyce led the way to the dock the next morning. The girl of the day before might never have been as she greeted both her and Joe with a sunny good morning. Unable to help herself, Summer's gaze flashed to Brandon's eyes, searching for something to deny the sinking feeling of loss in the pit of her stomach. The sea-green depths were as calm as the ocean around them—not a ripple of emotion disturbed their surface. His greeting was friendly without the slightest hint of awareness for her.

Summer turned away, glad for the necessity of remaining on the flybridge to run the boat.

"I can't wait to get started," Amy exclaimed, tossing Summer an excited grin. "Do you think there's a chance I may catch something? I've never even held a pole!"

Summer forced a smile, unwilling to spoil the bubbling brunette's fun. "There's always beginner's luck. Besides, from what I heard yesterday, it will be impossible not to catch something."

"What do you think the odds are of landing a marlin?" Chuck asked, matching his wife's anticipation.

Summer shrugged lightly as she headed for the ladder and her perch. "I'm not promising, but we'll do our best." Casting a quick glance over her shoulder, she saw Brandon, his arm around Joyce's bare shoulders, pointing out some of the various bits of tackle. The blonde's tactics appeared to have succeeded.

As Summer started the engines her mind automatically stowed her emotions away while the business of earning a living took over. She was too good at what she did to allow anything to deter her from giving her best. Being a woman in a basically male field had made her conscious of how much more proficient she had to be than the average man.

And the sea was a hard taskmaster, crueler than any human boss. It was a demanding mistress wanting total attention. Anything less and she was swift to retaliate. Summer knew this and accepted the challenge. There was a hazardous excitement in pitting her knowledge and experience against the elements at variance with the sense of peace and continuity in the ageless existence of the sea.

Summer lifted her face to the early morning sun, feeling the salty breeze in her hair, smelling the open ocean before her. She eased the throttle forward as the *Sea Mist* surged over the clear blue-green Atlantic.

On the deck, Joe was busy rigging the baits, his hands deft as he set bead rigs in one ballyhoo after another. Amy followed his movements with fascination.

"Why do you wrap that wire around the fish's bill?" she wanted to know as he set aside yet another bait fish.

"So it'll keep its mouth closed. Makes it troll better," he replied patiently, not pausing in his task.

"What's trolling?"

"The cap'n eases along"—he gestured toward the rods suspended over the gunwales in their holders— "and we toss the line out and tow the bait like this." He held the small fish up to demonstrate. "To a larger fish he looks like he's swimming. The big 'un comes by, takes a bite and hooks himself. Then Summer maneuvers the boat to keep the stern to the fish while one of you reels in the catch."

Amy beamed. "That sounds easy enough. How do you tell where they are?"

Joe glanced up, a twinkle in his eye. "We spy on them."

Returning the rod he had chosen for his own to its holder, Chuck came over and squatted down on his haunches beside his wife's seat.

"What he means is the captain has a white-line depth recorder that marks the school for us," he elaborated knowledgeably. "Then it's a matter of dropping the bait in front of its nose and hoping they're hungry."

"But they don't have a chance," she argued in disgust. "That's not fair."

Chuck and Joe exchanged man-to-man grins. "Just wait, honey, until you've got one on your hook and tell me that."

"Why?" she demanded suspiciously, glancing from one to the other.

"Why what?" Brandon echoed as he, with Joyce at his side, joined the group.

"We were explaining to Amy about angling," Chuck answered. "She's decided we're cheating by using so much equipment."

"Really, Amy, act your age. You eat seafood, don't you?" Joyce added dampeningly. She ran her hand down Brand's arm. "I can't wait to try my luck."

"That's a change," Amy observed with something of a snap, eyeing the other girl. "I could have sworn I

78

heard something about your being against this whole trip."

Chuck reached for her clenched fingers, shooting her a warning glance.

Ignoring Amy's anger, Joyce smiled complacently, her voice a purr as she spoke. "Brand persuaded me I would be missing a lot if I didn't join him."

Her double-edged comment effectively silenced anything Amy might have said. For a second no one spoke.

"We've got a school, Joe," Summer called from her perch. "It might be kingfish, or maybe dolphin."

"Let's get at it." Joe stood up, gathering his extra rigs.

Summer slowed the boat, easing past the schooling fish to make a wide swing around. By the time she was in position Joe had the lines out and the outriggers set.

They were halfway through their first run when the zing of the racing line popping loose from the outrigger warned that the bait had been taken.

"I got one!" Amy squealed excitedly, grabbing for her rod. "What do I do?"

Joe was beside her in an instant, calmly giving instructions. Then the other rigger snapped as Chuck's line tautened.

Amy reeled quickly as the fish raced for the boat. Just as the rod tip bent toward the water, the sleek iridescent blue and yellow body of a large bull dolphin broke the surface. Blunt-nosed, his short sail flying, he arced across the surface before diving deep for his freedom. Surprised by the power of the beautiful creature, Amy was momentarily stunned by the strain on her arms. She groaned as she hauled back on the rod.

"You don't have a winch, do you?" she panted, still reeling.

"Nope, that's not fair," her husband answered in between breaths from the other deck chair.

It was a good twenty minutes before they boated their prizes.

"Hey, Captain, you're right about beginner's luck—mine's bigger than Chuck's," Amy called when her fish was brought aboard. "I can't believe this is a dolphin. I thought it would be a porpoise, like Flipper, not this beautiful fish."

Summer grinned, acknowledging Amy's proud expression. "Ready for another go?"

"Have mercy!" she cried, easing her aching shoulders. "I'm sitting this one out. Joyce and Brand are going to try their luck."

The second pass was a repeat of the first except, predictably, Brandon landed a mammoth fish that turned out to be the biggest catch of the trip.

The sun was almost directly overhead by the time Summer eased into the mooring slip once more. As far as fishing went it had been a successful trip. Joe would have plenty of fish to clean and ice down, freezing them for the trip home at the end of the charter. The only discordant note of the morning had been when Joe gaffed Joyce's last haul of the day. Excited by the contest that had sprung up among the four of them, she had been right at the mate's elbow as he tried to drag her dolphin aboard. One final struggle for freedom had showered them both with sea water. Her squeals of outrage were drowned by their laughter over her drenched hair and sopping clothes. When Joe unthinkingly handed her the towel he'd been wiping his fishy hands on, that was the last straw. Joyce, reeking strongly of ballyhoo and sticky with salt spray, retreated to the cockpit chairs nursing her ill temper.

She was the first one off the boat. "For God's sake, hurry! I can't wait to get cleaned up," she complained, waiting impatiently for Brandon. "I have got to get out of this stinking mess!"

He eyed her sodden figure in exasperation. "So you've said—more than once."

Amy clambered up onto the dock, ignoring her husband's hand. "For goodness sakes, it's only water." She stood beside Joyce, catching a whiff of a distinctly fishy smell. Her nose wrinkled. "Oh, you do need a bath," she admitted with a giggle. She couldn't help but enjoy Joyce's discomfort. For once the glossy model-girl image was decidedly frayed.

A surge of red colored Joyce's pale skin as she glanced away from them. She caught Summer's sympathetic smile and the anger erupted. "It's all your fault. I bet you told that . . . that person," she pointed at Joe's sturdy figure, "to do it."

"That's enough." Brandon's harsh command sliced through her tirade. No one was smiling now. "You will apologize," he ordered in a tone that brooked no argument.

She stared at him, unable to believe her ears. "You're taking her side?" She tugged out the ends of her ruined silk shirt, holding it away from her body. "Just look at this. I'll never be able to wear it again. And it's her doing."

Brandon grabbed her by the shoulders, totally ignoring the rest of them. "I told you when we got up this morning to wear something casual. But no, you had to go looking like a nautical fashion plate." He gave her an ungentle shake. "It was your choice."

The small glow of warmth Summer felt at his quick leap to her defense faded at his verbal confirmation of Joyce's place in his life. She discovered that believing Joyce shared his bed and having him announce it to the world were two different things. She watched with self-punishing attention as the blonde collapsed against his broad chest, the muffled murmurs of contrition audible even to her ears. The sight of his arm curling around her shoulders as he turned her toward the path to the hotel was further proof. There was no apology. He had obviously forgotten her presence.

"Come on, girl," Joe prompted, catching sight of her expression. "Let's get this gear stowed away."

Summer pulled herself together at the concern in his faded eyes.

"We had better go on up," Amy said in a quiet voice. She was at a loss to explain the scene they had witnessed. "It was a lovely day," she offered, hoping to smooth away Joyce's insult.

Summer nodded, sympathizing with her embarrassment. Amy was a friendly girl and she liked her. "We'll see you tomorrow, same time."

After they left, Joe and Summer worked in silence, cleaning and preparing the boat for the next day's trip. Finally everything was shipshape.

"I think after lunch I'll do some snorkeling," Summer decided as she joined Joe on the dock. She fell into step as he headed for Salty's place. "What about you?"

"Not me. I'm pooped. I'll probably stay here, shoot the breeze and kill a few beers." He held the screen door open for Summer to precede him.

At first glance Salty's was no place special: a square white building on a lot sprinkled with a few weeds. Inside, the picture changed. A gathering spot for charter captains and crew, it boasted some of the best seafood on the islands. It was run by a retired captain with his wife as cook.

Noontime was always crowded, so Summer and Joe stood just inside the door as they searched for an empty place.

"Hey, Summer, over here." A booming voice rose above the babble and the clatter of silverware on china.

Summer followed the sound to the far corner booth and the burly figure of Jigger, a local fleet boat captain.

She smiled as she threaded her way between tables, answering greetings as she went. She slid onto the vacant bench, followed by Joe.

"This is Gerry." Jigger pointed to his companion. "That's Captain Summer and her mate, Joe."

Summer nodded, already surveying the menu. She missed the newcomer's surprised expression. "I think I'll have the conch fritters," she decided, naming a favorite island dish. She glanced up, catching Gerry's eye.

"Are you really a captain?" he asked, his tone indicative of his disbelief.

Summer eyed him, at her side feeling Joe's silent amusement. He couldn't have been more than twenty, if that. So new to the business he almost squeaked. "Yes," she answered simply, stifling the twinge of annoyance she felt at his masculine appraisal.

And his was the generation of women's equality. Each time it happened—as it always did when she announced her occupation—she told herself she shouldn't let it bother her. But it did. She would have to try to ignore the sensation of being a lone fish in a school of sharks.

Some of her irritation must have shown because Jigger didn't make his usual teasing remarks about how popular her charters were. "You going out again this afternoon?" he asked when the waitress had taken their order.

"Nope." Seeing his puzzlement, she explained. "Two of my passengers are women, and one's not too excited about fishing." That was putting it mildly.

"What a waste!" He shook his head. "Some people got more money than they got sense. I heard your guy was rich, but I didn't hear he was stupid, too. What did he hire you for if he was only going fishing half a damned day?"

Summer mentally winced at the word *stupid*. He was definitely not that. She shrugged. "It's his money."

"So what you gonna do with the rest of the time?" he asked as the waitress arrived with their drinks. She placed another beer in front of Jigger.

Summer took a swallow of her tea before replying. "I thought I'd do a little snorkeling and laze around. It isn't often I get the chance."

"Too bad I have to work or I'd come with you," Gerry offered, glancing at his boss.

"Nothin' doin'," was the uncompromising reply. "We have a full load and I need every man."

Summer was more than grateful for her friend's intervention. She was in no mood for young opportunists.

Suddenly she felt every one of her twenty-eight years. She found the youthful face boring. There were no lines to give it strength and character, no silver hair at the temples to lend it distinction. Even the brown soulful eyes were wrong. They should have been sea green. She pulled herself up short, realizing where her thoughts headed.

She stared down at the plate in front of her, scarcely hearing Joe's low rumble as he and Jigger swapped gossip. What had she been doing? Was she crazy? Was Brandon's face destined to impose itself on every man that bore even a slight resemblance to him? She hoped not. It was too ghastly to consider.

5

⠶⠶⠶⠶⠶⠶⠶⠶⠶

After spending a leisurely afternoon exploring the sea floor off a conveniently deserted beach, Summer was once again ready to face seeing Brandon and his favorite blonde. By dint of having supper in her room, she had avoided being an unpartnered fifth at dinner. Her carefully constructed poise was wasted when only three passengers stepped aboard.

"Joyce isn't coming," Brandon explained, his tone giving nothing away. "Shall we get started?"

Those words set the pattern for the next few days as each morning Brandon and the Bartos arrived promptly on the dot of eight. They fished, they laughed and joked, then returned to the dock early each afternoon sun-flushed and laden with their catches. The hotel freezer where they stored their catch until they were ready to leave was filling rapidly.

By the end of the third day, Summer had adjusted to Brandon's presence. The hours away from the blonde's influence gave her a chance to get to know other facets of his personality—his patience with Amy's amateur efforts at angling and the surprising friendship growing between him and the usually taciturn Joe. Toward her he remained friendly, even teasing, yet not once stepping across that invisible line of awareness of her as a woman. Though slightly piqued at his attitude, she was grateful for the respite. She desperately needed time to come to grips with her own body's sudden awakening.

The life she had led before her marriage had given little opportunity for a normal female awakening. Having no mother and being thrown into an almost totally male society, she had never had a chance for the usual boy-girl relationship. Then there was Tom.

Their love had been a gentle thing—almost an extension of the love she had felt for her father. Although deeper, it had been no preparation for what she was now feeling. Nothing that had gone before taught her how to deal with the instant awareness she felt whenever Brandon was near, the haunting quality of his sea-colored eyes or the breathless shock of his touch. Inexperience and fear made her fight her feelings instead of trying to understand them. She wasn't ready yet to put a name to them. And if she were, what would she choose? Loneliness? Desire? Love?

Since the first night she had managed to avoid any contact with her passengers except on board the *Sea Mist*. Considering the size of the island, that had taken some planning. Apparently her tactics had been noticed. Amy's stubborn insistence that she join them for dinner was impossible to ignore.

By the time she dressed in one of the only two long dresses she had packed, she had considered and discarded at least three excuses for changing her mind. As she surveyed her image in the mirror, she wished she were more imaginative. The memory of Joyce's voluptuous figure was too vivid for comfort.

She ran a hand over her hip, smoothing an elusive wrinkle from the soft tangerine lawn of her dress. She

eyed the camisole top with its delicate shirring support-
ed by the slender ribbon ties across her shoulders
doubtfully. She was woman enough to appreciate the
subtle peach tone against the honey gold of her skin,
but the style . . . ? What had made her buy it, anyway?
It certainly wasn't suitable for a widow with an eight-
year-old daughter. She didn't know how appealing the
fragile air of innocence was, coupled with her own basic
sensuality. She turned to check her travel clock, intend-
ing to change.

"Damn!" she swore softly, seeing the time. It would
have to do. She'd be late if she didn't leave. The last
thing she wanted was to be accused of making an
entrance.

As she entered the dining room she saw at a glance
she needn't have worried. She spotted Chuck and Amy
at a table by the glass windows overlooking the spot-
lighted pool and gardens, but there was no sign of her
host or his girlfriend. She threaded her way between
tables, totally oblivious to the interested male eyes that
followed her progress.

"I hope I'm not late," she murmured apologetically
as she sat down.

"Not at all," Chuck responded with an easy smile.
"We're early. Joyce and Brandon will be along in a
minute."

"I love that outfit." Amy's eyes reflected her sincere
praise.

Summer gazed at her gratefully. The petite brunette's
compliment eased her doubts slightly. "I wasn't sure it
was right," she admitted. "But it was a question of this
or nothing."

Chuck grinned on hearing the age-old female complaint. He, like his wife, had taken a liking to this
unusual woman. "Where have I heard that before?"

They both laughed at his teasingly disgusted tone.

"Heard what?" Unnoticed, Joyce and Brandon stood at the table.

Summer glanced up, looking straight into Brandon's eyes. Was it admiration she saw before he lowered his lids and turned to the girl at his side?

Her gaze moved reluctantly to his companion. Her startled gasp was covered by Amy's outspoken reaction.

"Good Lord, Joyce!"

In an atmosphere where casual elegance was the keynote, the blonde's outfit was anything but. It wasn't so much the dress as the way it clung to every lush curve of her body. Virginal white silk draped from one shoulder low across full breasts to be caught at the waist by a diamond clip. It rested mere inches above a seductive side slit revealing long golden legs.

Joyce slipped into her chair, a smile of mingled triumph and satisfaction lifting her lips.

"Have you ordered?" she asked in a husky purr, barely nodding a greeting to the silent Summer.

"We were waiting for you," Chuck answered.

Right on cue the waiter appeared, depositing a menu in front of each of them. Summer fixed her eyes on the elaborate card in her hands, trying to ignore Joyce's soft murmurs in Brandon's ear. Unable to resist a peek through her lashes, she was surprised and slightly comforted to see how little the blonde's enticingly packaged figure seemed to affect him. In fact, if she had to describe his reaction, she would have said amused.

As dinner progressed she found her appraisal was more accurate than she possibly could have guessed. While he did nothing to stem Joyce's definitely possessive, kittenish behavior, he didn't encourage it, either. When Joyce would have ignored her presence, he firmly drew her into the conversation.

Summer couldn't decide whether she was glad or

sorry. By the time the dessert dishes were removed she debated how to gracefully excuse herself.

Brandon's repeated refusal to respond to Joyce's advances coupled with his polite but definite interest in another woman had strained the blonde's smile and narrowed her eyes with rising temper.

Even Amy and Chuck weren't immune to the rapidly building tension. Summer noticed the uneasy glance her friend cast occasionally in Joyce's direction, and Chuck looked disgusted. Only Brandon was unaffected, his eyes unreadable in the softly lit dining room alcove.

The tuning up of the dance band came as a welcome diversion. In a few minutes she could leave, Summer decided gratefully. She knew the other four had planned on staying for a while.

"Joyce, I thought I saw you." The gay greeting was delivered with a New England twang, drawing everyone's attention.

"Sylvia . . . and Jeff," the blonde returned with a smile, catching sight of the slender, fair man behind her. "What are you doing here?" She raised an eloquent hand.

"Jeff was fishing, and I decided to stop off on my way home so we could return together," the new arrival explained easily. "Traveling with one's brother may not be the ideal, but it's definitely better than being alone."

The young man in question grinned good-naturedly. "What she means is I can do all the work while she sits around looking beautiful." Seeing only two familiar faces, he proceeded to introduce himself and the pretty auburn-haired girl at his side. "I'm Jeff Worthington and this, as you gathered, is my sister, Sylvia."

Brandon rose, dwarfing Jeff in both height and sheer power. Summer found herself comparing the two men.

"Will you join us?" he offered.

She watched Sylvia smile with pleasure. A quick

gesture summoned the waiter and two extra chairs. In the jumble of squeezing together around the circular table, Summer found Jeff placed between her and Amy with Sylvia on the other side of Joyce. Being partnered with the new arrival didn't bother her, but the fact that she sat jammed up against Brandon did. Every move he made, almost every breath he took, was instantly transmitted to her. She needed to escape from the heavy pressure of his thigh against hers, but there was nowhere to go.

The conversation drifted slowly at first. Clearly, if Joyce's expression was anything to go by, she was no happier with the inclusion of Sylvia and her brother, Summer thought with inner amusement. Even the talkative Amy was silent as she picked up the byplay of the two girls vying for Brandon's attention.

"When are you leaving?" Sylvia asked. "You know the party's in just a few days."

Joyce's voice took on a slightly waspish sting. "Not for ten more days. If I can't persuade Brandon to leave, we're going to miss it."

Summer saw Brandon's eyes narrow, but he made no response.

"You can't be serious, Joy," her friend exclaimed. "It's the biggest get-together of the season. Everyone will be there. They have a top-name entertainer and his entire band flying in from Vegas just for the occasion." Sylvia went on to highlight the star-studded guest list.

"Would you like to dance?" Jeff's low-voiced question caught Summer by surprise.

She glanced up to see him leaning over her and eagerly got to her feet. As she followed him to the small, glassy-smooth floor, she felt guilty for viewing his invitation as an escape, but not so much that she could refuse it.

Once there, she threw herself into the music, allowing

it to work out some of the tension that had built within her. Jeff was a willing partner, responding to her naturally graceful movements.

She loved dancing even as a child. She considered it one of her few truly feminine accomplishments—not that she had a great deal of time to indulge herself. They were both laughing and breathless by the time the swinging beat eased into a slow number.

Jeff took her in his arms without a word, taking her agreement for granted. Reluctant to go back to the table, Summer let him.

She felt none of the awareness she knew with Brandon as she brushed against his body. He was a good dancer and a pleasant man, but that was all.

She noticed Amy and Chuck joining the throng on the floor, and she couldn't resist a glance at their table. She watched as Sylvia excused herself and headed for the powder room.

"Are you really a captain?" her partner questioned curiously.

She nodded absently, her eyes fixed on the remaining couple. Even from her distance she could see that Joyce was furious. When the music ended she didn't want to return to the storm she sensed was brewing, but Jeff's hand on her waist propelling her off the floor allowed her no choice. It was impossible to miss Joyce's raised voice as they approached.

"Why won't you take me?" Joyce demanded, infuriated at his calm, almost indifferent refusal. "What possible difference can three or four days make?" Her eyes flashed angrily as she stared at him.

"You knew about the McFadden's party before you decided to come. If you had wanted to go that badly, you never should have agreed to join me," he returned reasonably. "Nothing says you can't leave when your friend goes."

Her lips tightened in rage. "You don't care, do you? After all this time, you still don't care. We're all the same, just another woman. No ties, no commitments, that's your philosophy to a tee," she said bitterly, her voice steadily rising.

"You're causing a scene," he murmured in warning, "and our guests are returning."

She glanced over her shoulder, seeing Summer and Jeff paused a short distance away. "Guests? That's another thing. I won't put up with that woman any longer."

Summer heard Jeff's swift intake of breath behind her. Much as she hated to be a witness to the scene, she had to stay. Jeff blocked her only retreat, and he showed no sign of stepping aside.

"You think I don't know you fancy her? What is she? The next trophy on your bedroom wall?" she demanded nastily. "Or is she already there?"

"Be quiet!" he stated through gritted teeth, his own anger flaring. "What I do, whether I sleep with someone or not, is my business, not yours. Keep your ugly suggestions to yourself." His eyes strayed to the motionless couple. He could tell by Summer's expression that she had heard Joyce's comments.

"If you want to go home, I'll gladly get you a ticket and take you to the airport," he offered quietly.

"That's right, get rid of me. I don't know why I came anyway. I thought it was just going to be the two of us. Instead you invited chaperones along. Then that beastly boat sank and we're cooped up on that little dinghy." Her voice shook with her sense of ill usage. "You haven't been near me since we left Boston. Every woman around gets more of your attention than I do." She fumbled for her bag as she pushed her chair back. "Well, I'm leaving. I've had enough. You don't even need to see me off. I'm sure Jeff and Sylvia won't mind doing the honors.''

Brandon rose to stop her as she turned on her heel and stalked angrily away. Then he shrugged, obviously remembering his other guests. A calm mask of politeness settled over his features.

Summer moved forward, urged by Jeff's hand at her back.

"I take it that she'll be leaving with us, Brand?'' he observed, apparently unmoved by Joyce's display of temper.

Brandon nodded. "If you don't mind." He still stood beside his chair, his attention now on the dance floor. "It looks like Amy and Chuck are returning." He glanced at Summer, his eyes expressionless as he met her gaze. "I had better go after her. Would you explain?''

"Yes," she agreed quietly. What else could she say? The flicker of gratitude in the aquamarine depths was curiously warming. She was aware of a singing sensation running through her. Joyce's angry accusation vibrated in her mind. He wasn't sleeping with her, and hadn't been!

Later, alone in her hotel room, Summer had the privacy she needed to examine her feelings. The rush of pleasure, the insane relief she had felt when she learned they had not been sharing a bed shocked her.

When had it begun to matter so much? And why did it? Brandon had never given her any reason to be jealous. And that's what it was—plain, old-fashioned, green-eyed jealousy. That's why she worried over her clothes, something she had never done before. She faced the fact that unconsciously she had wanted to exchange places with the blonde. For the first time in her life, she knew what it was to want a man to notice her. It was a frightening thought. She stared into her mirror as she creamed her face with moisturizer. Did it show, this growing ache inside her? The clear tawny eyes, the smooth unlined brow were the same as always. She breathed a sigh. Thank the stars she was spared that humiliation.

Summer half expected to see only Amy and Chuck coming down the hotel path the next morning. Brandon's tall, striding figure brought a slight smile to her lips, which she carefully camouflaged in her greetings to the three. It was almost nine, and although Brandon had called to say they would be delayed, he had not explained why. As usual, Amy was quick to announce the reason.

"Had you given us up?" she questioned with a grin as she bounced onto the *Sea Mist's* deck. "Joyce couldn't get an earlier plane, so I hope you'll forgive us. Chuck's about to foam at the mouth with impatience as it is. He's sure today is the day he catches his marlin.

Summer grinned. "So you feel lucky, Chuck?"

He nodded. "I do."

His wife cast him a teasing look. "Maybe I'll beat you out and catch your prize myself."

Summer caught Brandon's eye, finding the amusement she felt at the younger couple's banter echoed there. He crossed to her side, leaving them arguing amicably.

"Those two make me feel old," he murmured. He stood near enough to touch her, watching the way the sun danced over her golden skin. The smile of enjoyment that lit her eyes and curved her lips found its way to his mouth.

"I know what you mean. It's hard to believe they're married," she agreed as she in turn made her own survey of him. The pale yellow knit shirt stretched across deceptively powerful muscles, highlighting his deepening tan, the tobacco brown shorts a perfect complement. He looked superbly fit and more relaxed than a man should after saying goodbye to a woman who meant something to him.

"You wouldn't believe he's one of the sharpest men in our Boston office. At work he's definitely a no-nonsense type."

Her brow raised skeptically as she saw the "sharp office executive" pat his wife playfully on the rear. "They act like two puppies let out of confinement."

"You ready, Summer girl?" Joe called from the bow.

Startled, she glanced forward, taking in her mate's dour expression as he stood holding the loose mooring lines. "I guess I'd better get to work," she spoke aloud, heading for the flybridge ladder.

"We'll get the stern lines." Brandon moved away, gesturing for Chuck to help him.

Minutes later the *Sea Mist* headed for the open water. They planned to go farther afield, something they had decided before coming in the day before. Chuck's continued enthusiasm for a trophy catch had dictated their choice. While both he and Brandon appeared serious about their sport, they released as many as they kept.

"May I join you?" Brandon's voice drew her attention to him standing halfway up the ladder. The wind whipped his thick sable hair, tossing a heavy wave across his forehead. He flicked it away with impatient fingers only to have it fall back again.

"Of course." She slid over, leaving room for him on the seat. A glance to the lower deck showed Amy and Chuck ensconced in the fighting chairs at the stern. "Don't tell me your battle scars are showing?"

He eased down beside her. "Not exactly. I just don't

like being an extra." He glanced at the tachometer and speedometer. "She really can fly," he observed.

"Want to run her?" she offered, suddenly realizing how it might irritate him to be in the passenger seat. Over the last few days she had learned from Amy how involved he was in his business. The newspaper's jet-set image was inaccurate according to her.

Although he came from a wealthy, prominent family and never would have needed to lift his hand to anything, he had, on completion of college, started a small equipment-rental agency. In a few short years he had expanded to overseas work. His corporation, now having four major international offices, handled the big machinery required for all types of heavy construction. It was a worldwide concern requiring not only expertise and knowledge of the problems involved in each special locality but also, in many cases, delicate political maneuvering, an area in which he was especially gifted. Summer found it easy to believe the stories Amy told her of his success.

He grinned, looking years younger. "I was hoping you would ask," he replied, sliding over to take her place when she stood up.

"Hold her steady on that heading." She gestured toward the compass. "In another few minutes we should be getting some action." She looked below, expecting to see Joe already poised near Amy, prepared to lend assistance if she needed it. The outriggers were up and set, but she didn't see him.

"Summer." Joe's low roar came from the cabin directly under her feet. "Can you come down here?"

Puzzled, Summer looked at Brandon questioningly.

"I'm all right if you want to see what he needs."

She nodded, quickly descending the ladder to the lower deck. She found Joe hunched over nursing his

96

right hand in his lap. The muffled oaths weren't clear enough to be distinguished, but they were eloquent.

"It took you long enough," he grumbled as she reached him.

"Let me see." She gently pulled his fingers open. The long silver shank of the fish hook protruding from his palm told the story.

"I laid the damned thing on top of the reel," he explained, gesturing vaguely in the direction of the large Penn on the floor at his feet. "I didn't want to step on it. I forgot it was there. I picked it up and jammed the hook in."

Summer hardly heard his disgusted explanation as she reached for the cutters in the open tackle box on the floor. She did hear his hiss of pain as she pushed the shank through until the barb showed enough for her to cut it off. Once removed it only took a second longer to withdraw the shaft, leaving only two puncture holes. After cleansing it with an antiseptic, she bandaged it carefully.

"Damned fool thing to do," Joe admitted gruffly when she had finished.

She grinned. "It's age creeping up on you. It makes you forgetful," she teased, standing up.

The high-pitched whine of the outrigger drew their attention a split second before Chuck's excited shout.

"I got one!" He grabbed for his rod quickly, ready to reel the minute the fish made his initial run for freedom.

"Damn," Joe swore softly as the coveted blue marlin broke the surface for the first time, his splendid blue sail flying as he "walked" the water on a vee-shaped tail.

"I'll get Amy's line in," Summer offered, hurrying to the girl's side. With Joe's hand out of commission, they didn't need to be fighting two of them at once. She spared a quick glance at the flybridge, seeing Brandon's tall figure braced against the console while he watched the stern and their catch.

Now was the crucial test for any captain. Getting the anglers to the fish was only half the battle. The delicate orchestration of movement between the fishing craft and its quarry was a feat that took patience and razor-sharp reflexes. One false move, and too much or too little tension on the fragile line that bound the fish, and their trophy would be free to swim back to the traceless depths of its home.

When she had Amy's rod back in its holder, she left Joe below beside the still straining Chuck. From the size of his marlin, it could be an hour or more until it was boated.

She paused halfway up the ladder, admiring the quick efficiency of Brandon's hands as he swung the *Sea Mist* to starboard to keep the stern facing the fish. The concentration on his face was intense, his reactions sure. She relaxed visibly, acknowledging his expertise.

The *Sea Mist* had only known two captains, yet she answered his commands perfectly like the lady she was. Summer finished her climb more slowly, easing into her place beside him. Although she was alert to relieve him if it became necessary, she felt no desire to demand the return of the controls. She was vaguely shocked at her own reaction.

She rarely ever allowed anyone to pilot the *Sea Mist*, not so much because she couldn't bear the thought of someone else in her place as the need to show no sign of feminine weakness in a man's world. It was odd that she felt no such threat with Brandon. The thought gave her pause. Why didn't she, when he, more than anyone, made her feel more intensely female than she had ever been? What a crazy time to be wondering about that, she chided herself.

Nearly an hour and a half later, she returned to the

lower deck to give Joe a hand in boating Chuck's prize. Chuck was jubilant.

"I don't believe it." It was at least the third time he had said the same phrase since they had brought the fish alongside.

"Where on earth are we going to put it?" Amy piped up, surveying the glistening deep-blue and gray specimen with dismay. "It will take up an entire wall."

"Great!" her husband exclaimed, completely missing her expression as he gazed proudly at his trophy.

Amy rolled her eyes skyward. "I give up. He's not listening at all," she muttered just loud enough for Summer, who was standing near her, to hear.

Summer grinned, her eyes lighting with mischief. She glanced at Brandon and back down to the girl at her side. "Why don't you suggest he put it in his office?" She could barely restrain her giggles at Amy's arrested expression. "I mean, after all, what good is having caught a monster like this if you can't show it off?"

The two women stared at each other in perfect understanding before dissolving into laughter.

"What's so funny?" Chuck demanded, looking over his shoulder as he stood beside the marlin's head.

Amy ignored his question as she stepped closer to lay a hand on his tanned arm. "I have this most marvelous idea . . ." she began in her best submissive-wife voice.

Seeing that Joe had everything under control, there was no point in lingering. Summer mounted the ladder, her lips still curved in a smile.

"You look like a well-fed cat," Brandon remarked as she sat down beside him. "What have you been up to?"

She chuckled. "Helping Amy find a place for Chuck's dream," she explained gravely, her tone in complete variance with her dancing eyes.

He studied her openly. "Why have I got a feeling I'm not going to like the answer when I ask where?"

"I dunno," she drawled as she glanced below to see Chuck's pleased expression. She saw him look their way. "But I think you're going to find out."

Comprehension dawned when he followed her gaze. "You didn't!" he muttered as Chuck headed for the ladder. He didn't have time for much more before his friend's head appeared beside them.

"Amy had the most fantastic idea!" he enthused, apparently not noticing his boss's resigned expression. "I could hang it in the office. There's room on that far wall. The colors would match perfectly."

Brandon stared at Summer, reading the wicked amusement in her golden eyes, the tantalizing lips quivering with suppressed mirth. "It's your office," he agreed without turning his head. "You can hang anything you want there."

Summer was caught in the current of sea-colored eyes. One tiny corner of her mind registered Chuck's excited thanks and his rapid descent. Her laughter died slowly, bringing a tingling awareness in its wake. When his fingers came up to stroke her jaw, she felt the strongest urge to turn her lips into his palm.

"I should apologize," he murmured softly, oblivious to the chatter from below.

Her eyes widened in puzzlement.

"I should have handed the controls over to you when you came back," he explained, his thumb making featherlike caresses down her throat. "Do you forgive me?"

She nodded before running her tongue across suddenly dry lips, seeing his eyes flicker with awakening desire. She felt rather than saw him lean toward her. He's going to kiss me, she thought without surprise. And I want him to, she noted in amazement. Her lashes lowered almost without her being aware of it.

100

Joe, her passengers, even the *Sea Mist* dissolved into nothingness at the first touch of his lips. She realized she had been waiting for this moment for days. His mouth, warm and firm, probed the softness of her lips before deepening to possess her more completely. The tantalizing touch of his tongue swirled her senses, and a warmth tingled along Summer's spine, trickling heat to each nerve ending. With a sigh lost in Brandon's mouth holding her so deliciously captive, she gave herself up to the spell he wove about them.

Tentatively at first, Summer explored the source of the ever increasing pleasure radiating through her, her lips softening, opening even more fully. She drank thirstily of the clean taste of him, their mouths the one electric meeting point. Her arms reached up to curl around his neck, to draw him closer, but before she could feel the hard length of him pressed against her, Joe's voice brought reality crashing back.

"Are we going to make another run?" he roared from the stern.

Her eyes flew open as Brandon drew away, the moment shattered.

He smiled, his lips twisted ruefully. "Shall we change places?" he asked as he stood up.

Summer felt the warmth steal into her cheeks. She glanced below in embarrassment, prepared to see three pairs of eyes staring at her. There was none—not even Joe was paying any attention.

"It's all right," he reassured her gently. "From their angle they couldn't see anything."

She sighed, her hands going automatically to the controls. "Thank goodness." It was a fervent prayer of gratitude.

"Lady, you're certainly good for my ego," he remarked lightly, leaning back in the seat.

Relieved at his easy banter, Summer relaxed slightly. "I don't think you need any help with your ego unless it's to carry it," she retorted.

He flashed his famous smile. "Maybe. Then again, maybe not."

She glanced at him sharply, struck by the odd note in his voice. But she could tell nothing from his expression.

During the trip back to the marina, Summer was conscious of a new deepening level of communication between them. It wasn't so much what they said—their conversation was mostly about boats—but the way their thoughts seemed to merge. It was as though, with Joyce's removal, the barriers were down at last.

By the time they had dropped Chuck's catch off at the mounter's it was late afternoon.

"What time can you be ready for dinner?" Amy asked when they stood outside the main building of the hotel.

Summer glanced at her watch. "About seven."

"I'll stop by your room," Brandon suggested. "I understand tonight it's a buffet at poolside—it will be difficult to find anyone once it gets started," he went on to explain before she could protest.

"Okay," she agreed with a smile, curiously pleased by his protective gesture.

"I'm hungry already," Amy giggled. "I know I've put on five pounds since we arrived."

Her husband eyed her with a wickedly theatrical leer. "But all in the right places."

"Give me strength," Brandon muttered, meeting Summer's sympathetic eyes. "Will you two go away somewhere and play?"

"Okay, boss." Chuck's psuedosolemn expression was spoiled by a jaunty wave. "On our way." He grabbed his wife's hand and hustled her down the path for all the world like two children.

"I must have had brain damage when I invited that joker along," he groaned. "He was a bit nuts in college, but marriage seems to have pushed him around the bend."

Summer chuckled, trying to imagine the polished sophisticate in front of her in school with the irrepressible Chuck at his heels. The image just wouldn't come. While he definitely had a sense of humor, he was by no means the cutup his friend was. Never for a moment did the cloak of command, the smooth cosmopolitan manner, waver. Summer almost believed he had been born that way.

"You know you don't mean that," she scolded him with a twinkle. His skeptical expression didn't fool her.

He stepped forward to flick a teasing finger down the bridge of her nose. "You will be ready on time?"

She nodded, deliberately ignoring the teasing glint in his eye. She was too conscious of the public nature of their position. Her lashes lowered defensively.

"You won't always be able to hide from me," he taunted softly just before he turned away.

She opened her eyes to follow his disappearing figure. The smooth supple grace of his stride was the very essence of his personality. Self-assured, confident, a man of strength and purpose.

6

Brandon knocked on her door promptly at seven. Summer glided slowly across the room in answer, her nerves suddenly taut. She took a deep calming breath before she turned the knob. So much had changed in a few short hours that she felt more than slightly out of her depth, disoriented.

"Mm, perfect," he greeted, stepping forward into the doorway.

Surprised, for she hadn't expected him to come in, she backed away.

He pushed the door shut behind him and then reached for her. His hands were firm against her bare shoulders, impelling her toward him.

As she looked up to demand an explanation, her words died in her throat. The admiration, the slumbering fire in his eyes were a visual caress. The momentary stiffness of shock dissolved under the warmth of his gaze. She waited in curious stillness for the slow descent of his lips.

The first brush was gentle, tentative, a seeking touch, leaving her faintly dissatisfied. She swayed into the solid muscled wall of his chest, her arms slipping up his back to his shoulders. Her mute surrender awoke an answering response as Brandon's mouth covered hers in a kiss that began as a continuation of the first but abruptly exploded into a persuasive, sensuous demand unlike anything she had ever known. For a moment she fought the power threatening to stifle her and then, to her astonishment, she found herself melting into his arms. Her lips parted irresistibly until the warmth of his mouth made her moan softly. Her whimper seemed to trigger a deeper need in him, and even as she molded herself to his long body the quality of his kiss changed.

One hand moved down her spine, pressing her intimately against his hardening desire. She gasped softly at the contact, allowing Brandon to delve deeper into the honeyed well of her mouth. She barely felt the cool air touch her skin as her top was eased carefully down to expose one swollen, silken, tan breast. Brandon's fingers closed on the erect rosy peak, tugging gently in a reminiscent sucking motion that fired a raging blaze of desire through Summer's body.

She felt dizzy, divorced from her surroundings. Only Brandon existed, the heat of his body against hers, the exquisite pleasure of his stroking touch. The room dissolved into a dark mist that was frightening. This fear, the out-of-control sensation brought her back to reality.

"Brandon, no! Let me go!" she begged, tearing her lips from his.

"Don't ask me to stop, darling," he whispered in a husky rumble as his mouth trailed fiery kisses along her jawline and then nuzzled her ear. "I've been waiting too long . . ."

"Please, Brandon," she protested weakly, her resolve drowning in the passionate onslaught. "You go too fast." Summer brought her hands around to wedge between their bodies. She pushed against his chest but couldn't budge him. Whether it was her struggles or the desperation she heard in her own voice she didn't know or care at that moment, but she got his attention.

He lifted his head to gaze down into her flushed face. She saw the passion fade from the sea-green depths to be replaced by an almost tender softness.

"Golden eyes, are you afraid of me?" He lifted a hand to gently smooth the tawny curls back from her forehead. "You don't need to be."

She shook her head. "I don't do this kind of thing," she began awkwardly.

He dropped a light kiss on her nose. "Don't you think I know that?" he asked with a gentle smile.

"I'm sure you do," she snapped tartly, pulling out of his embrace. "That's the whole point."

He studied her carefully, making no effort to stop her from moving away. "Does it bother you?"

"No. Whom you sleep with is your own business, but I won't be one of your women." She watched his face close up, the eyes becoming cloudy, obscuring his thoughts. She felt his mental withdrawal and could have cried for the loss. She stiffened, angry at her body's traitorous need.

"Okay," he agreed calmly. "I've been warned off. Shall we go down?"

Disconcerted by his easy acceptance, she didn't move for a second. One dark brow quirked expressively, making her aware she had been staring. She reached quickly for her evening bag and crocheted shawl and allowed him to escort her from the room. The elevator ride to the lobby was accomplished in total silence. Summer wasn't sure whether to be glad or sorry about her escape. One part of her wanted more than anything to say the devil with her scruples and give in to the rising tide of feeling. The other more realistic side knew she couldn't handle the type of relationship he excelled in.

Chuck and Amy were already in the lounge. "We were beginning to think you had changed your mind about joining us," Amy greeted them as Summer slid into the booth.

"Not a chance," she murmured with determined cheerfulness. Not for anything did she intend to betray her chaotic feelings. The pressure of Brandon's thigh against her leg was doing things to her already shaky equilibrium.

"What will you have?" Brandon's cool voice was in sharp contrast to the earlier rich inflection.

"A bourbon and ginger ale." Suddenly she felt the need of something soothing. She was an infrequent drinker.

When he'd given their order, he relaxed in his seat, stretching his arm casually across the back of the bench.

"Now that you've captured your trophy, what would you like to do tomorrow?" he asked, eyeing his friends across the dimly lit table. "More fishing? Or have you had enough?"

Chuck glanced at his wife. "Amy wants to look around a bit, but how did you know?"

The waitress appeared with their drinks, momentarily forestalling his answer.

Brandon picked up his glass and took an appreciative sip.

"He probably heard me muttering," Amy chimed in with a grin. "I've loved the angling"—she shot a slightly triumphant look at her husband at the use of the more professional term—"but I would adore seeing more of these islands. I never knew anything could be so beautiful and relatively undeveloped."

Summer, pleased at the turn of the conversation, joined in. "It's amazing how little there really is in comparison to the large number of cays. Everyone hears so much about Nassau and Freeport that they

107

tend to think that's all there is. Personally I much prefer the out-island atmosphere, the deserted beaches, the unspoiled landscape.''

"Isn't it the truth," Amy agreed. "I know I expected something like Miami or Honolulu—traffic, tourists, shops, the whole thing.''

"So what would you like to see first?" Brandon asked, returning to his original question.

"How about Nassau? That is, if it's not too far away?" Amy asked hesitantly.

"I don't believe it. After what you just said, why do you want to go there?" her husband wondered.

"To shop, of course, and to sightsee. How can I go home without stopping there?" she returned with unassailable feminine logic.

Brandon turned to Summer. "Well, Captain, what about it?"

She shrugged lightly. "That's no problem. If we leave early in the morning, we'll be there by noon at the latest. We'll need to stay overnight, unless you three decide you would rather fly.''

"What do you mean three?" Amy demanded. "You're coming too, aren't you?" She glanced at Brandon. "Tell her."

Summer interrupted hastily. "If you go by plane, there's no need for me to come with you.''

"Look, why don't we argue this out over dinner," Brandon decreed, signaling for their check.

"Good idea. I'm starved even if no one else is," Chuck agreed, getting to his feet.

Summer and Amy walked together, leaving the men to follow behind.

"Don't you want to come with us?" her friend asked curiously. "I thought you liked us."

"I did . . . I do," Summer amended quickly, maybe too quickly, seeing Amy's sharp look.

"Then it's Brandon. Has he upset you?"

"Of course not," she denied as they stepped outside. "I just don't want to intrude. After all, I hired out as a charter captain. I'm not a guest to be entertained."

"Don't be ridiculous. If we didn't want you along, we wouldn't have invited you," Brandon argued brusquely. His hand gripped her elbow, drawing her toward the heavily laden buffet tables set up along the edge of the patio. "Let's see if some food can help your perspective."

Soft colored lights strategically placed in the lush foliage added a festive air to the poolside gathering. The lilting tones of island music was a perfect backdrop to the softly scented breezes and swaying palms.

Summer picked up a gayly patterned plate, making her way from the luscious pink-veined jumbo shrimp on their beds of ice to pale yellow pineapple, papaya and red strawberries, crab meat salad, steaming lobster tails, fried conch fritters and green turtle soup, an island delicacy. By the time she reached the end of the line she had a heaped plate, although she had chosen small portions of only her favorites.

Brandon eyed her full hands. "At least you don't feel obligated to pretend to be on a diet," he teased with a grin.

Summer sighed ruefully. "You're no slouch yourself," she retorted, glancing pointedly at his loaded platter. She was relieved at the return of his friendly banter. The passionate interlude might never have happened.

"There's a lot of me to fill up," he murmured wickedly as the Bartos joined them.

From then on the rest of the evening flew by. Brandon was his most charming, but without the sensual overtones expressed earlier. Summer found herself relaxing and enjoying the easy relationship between her passengers. Over dessert they finally decided to fly to Nassau and stay the night as well.

"I can't eat another thing," Amy groaned as she pushed her empty plate away. "In fact, I'm not even sure I can walk."

"And here I was going to take you dancing," her husband suggested disappointedly.

She shook her head. "No way am I going to let you drag me onto that floor right now. Your idea of dancing is not mine," she returned, referring to his enthusiastic approval of everything except the waltz.

"You two can sit here and argue all night as far as I'm concerned. Summer and I are going in. The music is too good to waste," Brandon stated, rising to his feet.

Under his commanding eye, Summer found herself out of her chair and allowing him to lead her through the open glass doors to the dance floor.

"You could have asked," she muttered as she moved into his arms in time to the slow music.

"Why?" he murmured against her hair. "You might have said no. This way I get you in my arms without a struggle."

Instinctively Summer stiffened at his calm announcement. Lulled by his easy manner and almost impersonal attitude during dinner, she had lost her wariness.

"Relax. What can I possibly do in the middle of a crowded room?" he chided softly.

"I don't know and I don't want to find out, thank you," she informed him tartly, her tone somewhat spoiled by the soft gasp of pleasure she gave as his lips traced the outline of her ear. The light caress sent shivers of delight across her skin. Unconsciously she moved closer.

He responded by pressing her tighter against his body.

Summer struggled briefly, then sighed. What was the

use? She was safe enough for the moment. Why not give in to her clamoring senses?

Brandon silently guided her around the floor, seemingly content just to have her in his arms. It was only when the band picked up the beat that he released her.

He gazed into her eyes, apparently oblivious to the people around them. "Do you feel like a walk on the beach?"

She stared back at him. Common sense told her to say good night now, yet she found the words wouldn't come. Instead she inclined her head slowly. Caught in his spell, she wasn't even able to resent the satisfaction in his expression as he led her unresisting past the patio tables to the flowered path leading to the shore.

The chatter of the guests and music faded into the background, the soft murmur of the sea lapping against the sand replacing it. The moon sprinkled silver glitter across the calm ocean as the path ended on a white stretch of deserted beach.

They stood for a moment beneath the feathery coconut palms, surveying the quiet splendor. Brandon's arm slipped around her waist, drawing her against his hip. She leaned her head against his shoulder, hearing the steady beat of his heart beneath her ear blending with the timeless rhythm of the sea. It seemed so right somehow.

When he turned her in his arms, she lifted her head to meet his lips as though impelled by a force outside her control. Expecting another passionate deluge, she was surprised by the gentle strength of his seeking mouth coupled with an obvious restraint. When he raised his head she found she was vaguely dissatisfied by the change. She searched his expression in the shadowed moonlight, but she couldn't read his eyes. They carried the same blank silver sheen as the ocean before her.

"Let's walk," he suggested softly.

"All right."

He looked down at her feet. "Will you be able to in those?" he asked dubiously, eyeing the slender white high-heeled sandals.

"It would be safer if I took them off." She bent over to unstrap them, accepting the support of his arm. "Shall I leave them here?" she asked when she had finished.

"I'll put them in my pocket." He held out his hand. "Ready?"

She placed her hand in his large grasp and allowed him to draw her out into the moonlight. The sand was warm beneath her bare feet, the breeze a pleasant drift of cooler air against her skin.

Neither spoke as they strolled side by side, leaving a trail of footsteps in their wake. It was as though they were the only two people in the world. When they came to the end of the tiny finger of land that marked the boundary of the cove, Brandon halted, bringing her around to face him. He took her free hand in his.

Summer stared up at him, his face plainly visible in the silvery light.

"You were right. I was rushing you. Maybe it's because I've been waiting so long. I'm not really sure," he explained, dispelling the silent interlude. He paused to study her face seriously. "Don't you feel it—the spark between us?"

For an instant Summer was startled by his frank discussion, especially in view of the romantic surroundings. Any other man, she felt certain, would have made use of nature's props and tried to overpower her objections. It was a measure of Brandon's sensitivity to her feelings that he did not.

"More like a bonfire," Summer commented with a

smile of self-mockery. There was no point in denying what he already knew.

He covered both her hands with his, pressing them against his chest until she could feel his heart beating. "I can't promise not to try to change your mind—I want you too much. But I will give you my word I won't sneak up on you. If we make love, it will be because you want it as much as I do."

She met his steady gaze, her eyes molten pools of emotion. The promise she saw reflected there destroyed any last lingering doubts she had about his womanizing reputation. He was attracted to her, a fact he made crystal clear, but he also was offering her a fighting chance—the knowledge he had given her against his undisputed expertise.

The demon in her rose to challenge. Realizing it was the response he probably expected, she still couldn't resist the unspoken dare. "I appreciate the warning."

Tawny eyes glittering with determination met the jade-green purposeful stare. The deserted beach became the arena for the most primitive battle of all: man against woman. Frozen in the moment, the adversaries weighed each other's weaknesses, the slender golden girl and her towering dark-haired champion.

Then Brandon lowered his head, his mouth seeking and finding Summer's upturned lips. The first clash in the battle was a tentative feint. Mastery of the male against the subtlety of the female. When it ended, as it did abruptly when Summer drew away, they were both breathless.

Brandon's chest rose and fell quickly. "Now you know."

"Now I know," she echoed between breaths. She was fully aware that he had let her go when he could have held her in his embrace. The urge to return to his arms was strong. She could feel his silent command to surrender, but she resisted its siren call. "Shall we go back?"

For a second he appeared to debate agreeing before he nodded once again, taking her hand. "You won't run away, will you?" he asked in a husky murmur, studying her profile. He traced the swollen fullness of her lips, which so recently had known his possession. He wanted her. He almost regretted his honesty. Yet he didn't. Her spirit was part of her allure.

She glanced at him under the thick screen of golden lashes. "No, I'm no coward. Foolish maybe, but not a coward," she returned quietly. She could almost hear his sigh of relief.

When they reached the path leading to the pool area, they nearly collided head-on with Chuck and Amy.

"There you are," the brunette exclaimed. "We were just coming to look for you." She eyed their clasped hands with satisfaction.

Summer tugged carefully at Brandon's hold but only succeeded in tightening his grip. Short of an undignified struggle she had no choice but to leave it there, suffering Amy's knowing look in the process.

"I have a super idea," her friend went on when no one commented. She looked to her host. "Since we have an extra bedroom now that Joyce is gone, why doesn't Summer move in with us?"

Brandon turned, meeting the appalled comprehension in Summer's eyes. "She may prefer her privacy, Amy," he explained in an expressionless tone, giving none of his own feelings away.

"I told you it was a crazy idea," Chuck said, gesturing helplessly.

"Well, you will admit it would save time. I mean, look at tonight. We could have gone straight in to dinner without waiting for Brandon to collect Summer." She glared at her husband before turning back to the other girl. "Besides, I would love to have some female company. Say you will," she pleaded.

Summer shook her head helplessly. How could she explain why she didn't want to join them. Logically, as far as Amy was concerned, there was no reason why she shouldn't. How could she admit she was afraid her determination would not survive in close proximity to Brandon's disturbing presence. She couldn't.

"I don't think it's necessary," she began in weak protest.

"Nonsense. What possible reason is there to pay for a room when you could use ours. Think of the convenience of all of us being in the same place." Amy's argument was irrefutable. "Say yes," she almost commanded.

"All right," Summer agreed reluctantly. She felt Brandon's fingers squeeze hers reassuringly. "It's been a long day. I don't know about the rest of you, but I'm for bed."

"Good idea," Chuck echoed, taking his wife by the arm. For all his kidding around, he was perceptive, especially where his best friend was concerned. He felt the tension between Brandon and the slender girl, and it didn't take two guesses as its cause.

When the other couple was out of earshot, Brandon spoke. "You don't need to accept if you would rather not," he offered quietly. "That was never part of the plan."

She nodded. "I know. You looked as shocked as I felt," she commented with a weak grin.

"Lady, I was. I could just see your hand connecting with my face." He shook the appendage under discussion gently. "And since I'm a gentleman, I wouldn't have been able to hit back."

"Gentleman?" she snorted, responding gratefully to his teasing. She vaguely sensed the expertise of his charm as he deliberately eased her fears. By the time they reached her room, Amy's suggestion had faded in importance. She could handle him.

His kiss was gentle against her lips as he reached behind her with one hand to push open the door. "Sleep well," he murmured softly. He trailed his fingers lightly down her throat before he released her.

With a last lingering look she went in, shutting the door quietly behind her. She leaned against it for a second, knowing he was just outside. The muted sound of his receding footsteps released her, and she moved toward the bathroom, dropping her bag and shawl in the chair on the way. The bed routine went by in a fog as Summer reviewed the events of the extraordinary day. When her head hit the pillow she was musing over her total belief in Brandon's word. With any other man she doubted she would have accepted such a guarantee. Yet with him she had no such reservation. She fell asleep smiling at the incongruity of his public image and the real man.

Summer surfaced groggily the next morning to the muffled sounds of knocking. She pushed her tousled hair from her eyes and glanced at her travel alarm. Her gaze narrowed as she read the early hour.

"Okay, okay, I'm coming," she muttered, crawling out of bed and groping at its foot for her yellow cotton robe. She pulled it on hastily as she padded to the door. "Who is it?"

"It's me, Amy," her friend answered cheerfully though ungrammatically through the closed panel. "May I come in?"

Summer turned the knob, releasing the lock.

"Good grief, did I wake you?" Amy asked in dismay. "I never thought!"

Summer waved her hand in a dismissive gesture. "It's

116

all right. I just forgot to set my alarm. You did me a favor, really."

Amy flopped down in her one chair, a grin on her face. "I came over to help you move," she announced to Summer's back as she crossed to open the drapes, letting the early morning sun pour in.

"What?" She stared over her shoulder at Amy's smiling face. "You've got to be kidding. What's the rush?" she demanded inelegantly.

"Our plane, that's what. I thought if I came over early, between us we could get you packed and out of here before we need to leave at nine o'clock. Brandon promised to see the office about the switch. And a porter will take care of the luggage."

"Were you a general in your past life?" she asked faintly, bewildered by the crisp air of command. She had the overwhelming feeling of being pushed into something willy-nilly. She had barely adjusted to the situation as it presently stood. All of her confidence of the night before seemed to desert her.

"No, just the mother of twin boys. Besides, I couldn't wait to have you join us so I won't be outnumbered." She giggled, making shooing gestures with her hand. "Why don't you get dressed while I get started?"

Summer headed for her closet, shaking her head in defeat. She was helpless against her friend's insistence. Short of hurting her feelings she had no choice.

By the time she had finished her shower and got into her clothes she found Amy snapping the last strap on her bags.

She looked up, a faint flush of exertion on her cheeks as Summer reentered the room. "All done," she announced in satisfaction. "I've even called the bellboy."

Summer managed a smile, masking her uneasiness. While in the privacy of the bathroom, she had had time to think. In the cool light of day all her doubts returned.

Could she withstand Brandon's attraction? She didn't know, and there lay the danger.

The cause of her seesawing emotions opened the door of the two-storied townhouse just as they reached it.

"Well, girls, your timing's excellent." He led the way to a luxuriously appointed living room overlooking a smooth stretch of beach.

Never having been in one of the ocean homes, Summer looked around her with interest. Overstuffed matching oatmeal sofas flanked one wall, facing the wide expanse of glass separating a small terrace from the living area. The cool, muted tones of the ice green walls and coral accent pieces successfully married the tropical outdoors with the comfort-oriented interior.

"Isn't it gorgeous?" Amy questioned as she noticed her appreciative gaze. "It makes you wish you could live here year 'round."

"You forget she does, love." Her husband entered from a door that could only lead to the kitchen since he carried two steaming mugs of coffee. He handed one to his wife before extending the other to Summer. "You can sit down," he teased with an easy grin, gesturing to a place on the couch opposite from where they stood.

"I think she's still asleep," Brandon said at her side. His voice carried an unmistakable hint of mockery, earning him a sharp look. He grinned into Summer's indignant eyes, enjoying the spark of irritation. "She hasn't even said hello yet."

"Hello, Chuck, hello, Brandon." She enunciated each word clearly before moving to take the seat Chuck indicated.

"Are you always this grouchy in the morning?" Brandon asked with a perfectly straight face as he took a place beside her.

Too late she saw the half-full mug on the low

glass-topped table in front of her. She lifted her own cup to her lips, her eyes meeting his over the rim. "Always—until I have my coffee," she murmured.

He raised his mug in silent acknowledgment of her thrust, a wicked gleam in his eye. She could see him storing her remark away for future reference.

"Bravo!" Amy congratulated. "I knew you would fit in. Finally I'm not going to be outnumbered."

"It would take an army troop to outnumber you, my love." Chuck again emerged from the kitchen in time to deliver his husbandly pronouncement.

Summer couldn't control the amusement at Amy's disgusted pout. Beside her she heard Brandon's deep-throated laughter. "Are you sure you want to risk this nuthouse?" he asked against her ear. "It might be infectious, you know."

She nodded turning her head to stare into the face so close to hers. For a split second she found herself drowning in the blue-green eyes with their tiny flecks of burnished gold. "It might be the nicest bug I ever caught," she murmured with a smile that said more than her words.

"We'd better get going, you two, or we'll miss the plane," Chuck warned with a glance at his watch.

"See, nothing to worry about, golden eyes," he muttered, rising and drawing her to her feet. "Chuck and Amy are the perfect chaperones."

Summer stifled the urge to grin at his thwarted tone. Brief though his foray into her defenses was, she was grateful for Chuck's intervention. It showed beyond a shadow of a doubt she was as safe as she wanted to be. The problem was . . . did she wish to be?

From the outset Brandon had made his attitude plain. Though he was subtly possessive, there was nothing in his manner to embarrass her or make her uncomfortable.

Their trip from Abaco to New Providence was smooth and all the avid Amy could have wished. From their seats facing each other in their twin-engined plane, they truly had a bird's-eye view.

Seen from above, the jewellike swirls of deep indigo blue, peacock and teal surged around various textured clusters of verdant green islands edged with distinctive white beaches. Here and there tiny specks of color nestled among the trees, indicating a house or two.

It was only when they circled Nassau itself that they saw the signs of modern-day technology. The checkerboard layout of white buildings interspersed with green trees rose from the north side of New Providence.

"It's so small," Amy exclaimed, craning her head to see it all at a glance.

Summer, too, had her eyes on the scene below. She saw the gleaming hulls of two luxury ships resting side by side in Nassau's deep-water harbor, port of call for many of the world's finest cruise ships.

"It may seem that way, but it is the capital," she explained, glancing back at her friend. "It's also the richest and most highly developed city in the islands. See that strip of land over there?" She gestured to the finger of green across the harbor. "That's Paradise Island. For many years it was reputed to have one of the best beaches in the cays, but without the usual string of hotels. Then it was called Hog Island by its owner, Dr. Winner-Gren—a weird name for such a beautiful place."

"So what happened?" Amy demanded.

"He built a house that later became the famous Ocean Club." Brandon took up the narrative. "After him came a man named Hartford who changed its name and started development. He finally sold out to the present resort chain."

"Is that where we're staying?"

He nodded, glancing at Summer. "Have you ever been there?"

"No, but I've heard a lot about it. There's a casino, too, isn't there?"

"Don't tell me you're a gambler?" he teased.

"Not me. I play it safe—haven't you noticed?" she answered back pertly, enjoying the double-edged mockery.

Sightseeing with Brandon was an experience, Summer found. He seemed to know by instinct what would please each of them. They began at the busy, colorful Nassau harbor with its fascinating floating market of sailing vessels, which brought in fresh fruit, fish, vegetables and conch every morning to the docks, finishing with the straw market, where Amy literally went wild.

At lunch he hired a horse-drawn carriage for the rest of the day. Settled beneath its gay canopy, with the steady clip-clop of hooves for accompaniment, they saw Government House atop Mount Fitzwilliam as well as the gracious, stately homes of old Nassau with their English estate charm of wrought-iron gates and well-groomed gardens. By the time they crossed the channel back to Paradise Island and their hotel, Summer and Amy were pleasantly exhausted.

"I don't think my feet will ever be the same again," Amy moaned. She sat slumped in a chair, her maltreated appendages propped on a convenient ottoman.

"I know what you mean," Summer grinned, rubbing her own toes in commiseration. "I thought I was in shape until I went with you two." She glanced at Brandon and Chuck where they stood chuckling at the picture the two women made.

"Well, you said you wanted to see—" Chuck began self-righteously.

"I know I did, but I never said all of it in one day," his wife responded.

"We carried the packages," Brandon pointed out, a strong tanned hand gesturing toward the small mountain of bundles on one end of the suite's sofa. "I didn't notice either of you offering to help with that."

Summer giggled. "You told me I could buy that hamper," she reminded him, referring to the largest square package.

He took the couple of steps needed to bring him directly in front of her chair. "I didn't mind that as much as the conch shells, and the other stuff that went along with it."

Feeling perfectly safe with Chuck and Amy in the room, Summer teased him. "But certainly you were strong enough to handle it?" she teased outrageously.

The gleam in his eyes told her he was going to retaliate, causing her glance to flicker. "And you, too, golden eyes," he whispered softly, his breath fanning her tousled mane of curls as he stood in a mock threatening position over her.

"Oh!" Amy's choked groan drew their attention.

Brandon straightened and stepped back.

"I don't know about the rest of you, but I think I'll lie down," she said feelingly. "What about you, Summer?"

Summer nodded, quickly getting to her feet.

"Don't forget to set an alarm or something, love," Chuck reminded Amy. "You won't have me there to do the honors."

Amy shot him an indignant glare. "It's not my fault Brandon could find only this suite. It won't kill you for one night to share a room, and there are the twin beds."

This was the busiest tourist season of the year, and it coincided with the annual Bahamas Flying Treasure Hunt, an event for private planes. The occasion lured hundreds of pilots and guests to the islands.

Across the room Summer met Brandon's eyes, glowing with a warmth that stirred tendrils of feeling to life.

"Summer and I could still share," he suggested.

Amy grabbed Summer's arm as though to hold her at her side. "You'll do no such thing, Brandon Marshall." Her voice and expression were the picture of outraged virtue, drawing a smile from her friend.

Summer's eyes said, "It serves you right," but she didn't utter a word.

Brandon inclined his head, acknowledging her retaliation with a grin. "We should leave about seven-thirty if we're to keep our reservations," he suggested. "Will you be recovered by then, Amy?"

Three hours later, Amy sat in front of her dressing table glumly surveying her deeply pink nose. "I look like Rudolph, the red-nosed rabbit."

Summer looked up from strapping on her white high-heeled sandals to stare at her roommate's bare back. From her position seated on the end of her bed she had an excellent view of the offending feature. "I think you've got your seasons scrambled," she observed, controlling a desire to laugh.

"Maybe, but I can't go out like this." She dipped her fingers into a small pot and dabbed a dark colored cream over the rosy area. "I did better on Treasure Cay."

"So did I," Summer murmured with feeling, thinking of the growing attraction between her and Brandon. Somehow it was much more difficult to stick to her resolve when she was free from the responsibilities of the *Sea Mist*. Today had been a space out of time. Shannon, Tom's Rest, Gussie and the boat were a life apart.

Catching a glimpse of her friend's expression, Amy turned, her eyes deadly serious. "You're not falling in love with him, are you?" she asked quietly.

Summer stared at her, hearing the mingled hope she wasn't and worry she was in her whispered question. For a moment she debated denying it.

"I'm sorry," Amy gestured helplessly. "I shouldn't have pried."

"No, it's all right, really." She studied her hands in her lap for a moment before raising her eyes. Amy was the closest she had ever had to a girlfriend. In spite of her teasing nature, she had a deep strain of common sense as well as being a surprisingly acute judge of character, which Summer respected. Amy's reaction to Summer's taciturn first mate and her attitude toward Joyce showed that. She, more than anyone, might be able to help her. "In a way, I'm glad you did." She laughed a little unsteadily. "At my age, you would think I could gauge my own emotions."

Amy noted the uncertainty with dismay, something she tried to hide but did not quite succeed.

"I know I'm crazy to even consider it. I've told myself often enough . . ."

"What about Brandon? Has he said anything?"

Her cheeks flushed as she remembered the scene on the beach. "He wants me, he's made no secret of it."

Summer saw the question in her eyes and continued. "I'm attracted to him . . . more than that." She paused awkwardly. "But that's all there is," she stated with desperate emphasis. "I'm not from his sphere. We have nothing in common at all." It was a plea.

Her friend's face was sad as she nodded her agreement. "From the world's point of view it's true, you don't." It was her turn to search for words. "When I met Chuck, I was working as a waitress in a coffee room. He made me feel so special, beautiful. But I was all wrong for him. He came from a good home, while I never knew my parents. He had the college education and a great job. I had only finished high school. He liked the theater and I had never even been—so many differences and yet we couldn't ignore the feeling between us." She stared across the space separating them.

"It was hard, more difficult than even Chuck realized. Oh, his friends were kind enough in front of him, but alone—that was something else again. None of it was deliberate. We just had nothing to talk about. Even now after four years I still find myself out of my depth occasionally."

"You married him knowing the hazards. I'm fairly certain Brandon hasn't got anything that permanent in mind," she admitted.

"Probably not," Amy agreed honestly. "At this point anyway." She saw the pain dim those extraordinary golden eyes. "But I'll tell you this. In all the time I've known him, I've never seen him behave with any other woman the way he does with you. He has lost that terribly polite sarcasm he usually employs. He's more like the real Brandon, the one we know."

Summer's brows rose skeptically.

"Besides, he can't keep his eyes off you . . . or his hands, either." A telling observation that drew a gasp from Summer.

"What do you mean?"

A couple of knocks sounded at their door, drowning out Amy's reply. "Hey, are you two finished yet?" Chuck called. "We're going to be late."

Serious conversation ceased as both girls scrambled into their dresses and collected their bags.

When they were ready Amy paused, her fingers on the door handle. "A man Brand's age doesn't normally haul a stack of packages around on a sightseeing tour, nor does he hold hands with a girl an entire day."

Summer's lips curved into a smile at the picture she drew.

"Think about it," Amy advised before opening the door.

As the women entered the living room the two men, attired in white dinner jackets and black slacks, stood against the miniature bar, a drink in front of each of them.

"They made it," Chuck announced in surprise, checking his watch.

Brandon's eyes roamed over Summer's form, admiration darkening the aquamarine depths. He finished his drink in one swallow before he spoke. "It was worth the wait." His smile encompassed both women, although it lingered on Summer.

Dinner was superb in the hotel's elaborately appointed restaurant. Afterward they made their way along the corridor that connected the hotel with the Paradise Island Casino.

After a few bets, Summer retired from the tables with Brandon at her side, leaving Amy with a steadily growing pile of chips still at it. Chuck stood at her elbow, encouraging her efforts.

"Would you rather sit down in here or shall we try the terrace?" Brandon asked, guiding her between the crowded green tables.

"Outside, please." The rapidly filling room and the voices of the wagering masses was claustrophobic, to say the least.

The cool breeze from the water greeted them as they stepped onto the virtually deserted patio. The darkness was lit by cleverly concealed colored lights. Brand led her to a soft-cushioned rattan seat built for two people.

"Is this all right?"

She nodded, enjoying the sudden peace. Brandon sat down beside her. It seemed right somehow when he put his arm around her shoulders and drew her against his side so invitingly close. Neither spoke, content for the moment to savor their haven. The awareness between them was as strong as ever, but the pressure of fulfillment was absent, almost as though there was a temporary truce.

"Did you enjoy today?" His question was soft, not intruding on the aura surrounding them.

"Yes. I can't remember the last time I did so many crazy things." Unknowingly, she portrayed more clearly a picture of her life than all the explanations in the world.

Brandon's arm tightened in a protective gesture. "You mean you don't go sightseeing with all the trips over?" he asked in a gentle teasing, covering a need to probe into this girl's past. Her curls tickled his cheek as she shook her head.

"No time, usually. In the off season there's still plenty to keep us busy. Boat and equipment maintenance plus the charters," she replied matter of factly.

"What about your social life? Surely you go out?"

In the darkness Summer missed the intensity of his gaze. His question appeared casual, so she had no hesitation in responding.

"Occasionally I do, but not too often. Gussie and Shannon provide me with plenty of company, and there's the rescue service radio to be manned. We have an emergency at least once a week."

Brandon's brows drew together in a frown as he pictured the bare starkness of her life. Everything about her shouted a working woman and mother: the short-age of evening clothes—he hadn't missed the fact that she alternated her after-five attire between two simple dresses—and the awe with which she viewed her surroundings. Was he insane to feel the way he did about this woman? She was so far removed from his background and the very values his world held dear. Who among his friends would even understand her or she them? People like the Bartos, maybe, but certainly not the Joyces of his existence. And unfortunately there were more of those than any other.

Curious at the stillness she sensed in him, Summer turned to catch the remnants of his thoughtful expression. "What is it?"

He glanced down on her upturned face. Even in the subdued lighting, her clear golden eyes held him spellbound. God, she was beautiful. Unable to help himself, he raised his free hand, his fingers gently tracing the contours of her cheeks, her jaw and finally her lips. His thumb trailed softly over the lush fullness until they parted, expelling a tiny puff of warm breath against his seeking probe. He lowered his head, drawn by the unspoken invitation. "I was thinking of you," he replied with husky truthfulness.

Summer saw his slow descent in something of a daze. When had the safe haven of peace changed? When had it become the sweet burning embers of desire flickering to life, spreading heat through her veins? She didn't know. She only knew she was helpless to hold back her response. She ached for his touch on a level beyond her mental control.

When it came, it was as gentle as the breeze against her skin. The tantalizing brush of mouth succeeded in drawing her closer to him in an attempt to prolong the light caress. The second kiss took what she was so ready to give as he exerted pressure to release the honeyed sweetness of her mouth and to explore its moist depths.

Barely aware of her own actions, Summer twined her fingers in the thick strands of his sable hair, her body arching closer to the source of the fire burning within her.

She forgot where they were, forgot everything but the clamor of her senses. Brandon's hands moved over her shoulders, down her spine until she was powerless to control the quivers of sensation running through her. Surrender was only a hairsbreadth away.

And then something changed. A subtle alteration in Brandon's lips, his touch and his body combined to draw her back to earth.

There was no harshness, only a gentle undeniable shift in that direction. He still kissed her, his fingers still trailed delight across her body, but she knew he was pulling her back.

The raging ache in her subsided to a soft warm glow. Her lips once again felt the taste of his mouth, undemanding of fulfillment.

"Are you all right?" His voice was a soft whisper.

She nodded, unable to speak. How quickly she had succumbed to his expertise, yet she felt no shame, no defeat. Even now as he eased her away from him she knew no rejection. Unexplainable as it was, she knew in that moment she loved him. The realization gave her a glow which Brandon's shrewd eyes could not miss.

"Ah, golden eyes," he murmured on a soft sigh, "if you only knew the power you hold."

"Do I?" she whispered, drinking in the sight of the moonwashed planes of his face, uncaring of the words she spoke. They were unimportant at this moment. She knew in her mind she only had a few short days of his life before he would leave, yet she wouldn't give up one second, nor regret her surrender when their time ended.

"Come." He rose, holding out his hand. It was almost symbolic.

She placed her fingers in his, content to follow his lead.

The strangeness, the sense of conflict no longer existed between them. As they stepped across the threshold back into the gambling room, they came face to face with Chuck and Amy.

"We've been looking for you," Amy greeted them, eyeing their clasped hands for a split second.

Summer smiled a slow, sweet curve of happiness. "We were outside," she explained simply.

Once Summer was in bed, with Amy occupying the other twin, her mind began to relive the last few hours. She knew now the instantaneous attraction between them was a strong, undeniable bond. She had fought a long, lonely battle and still the chemistry between them burned as fiercely as ever. She knew without Brandon telling her that he, too, had not succumbed easily. They were meant to share this time together. It was a fact as inevitable as the coming satisfaction and fulfillment of their final joining. Each step, each act had been as predictable as the changing tide and, as with the tide, unrelenting. She still had time to turn aside before the final commitment, but she wouldn't. Her decision was made.

Perhaps back home where Shannon might be hurt by cruel gossip her answer would have been different. Even then she wasn't sure. But here it was different. There was no Gussie, or Shannon to worry. Only Joe and he, she knew, respected her privacy. He had said his piece and would say no more.

She slept soundly for the first time in days, untroubled by dreams of pursuit. Her flight was over.

7

The certainty of her actions stayed with her as Summer arose the next morning, clear-eyed and smiling. Amy's groggy expression when she stepped out of the bathroom wrapped in a towel made her laugh. What a beautiful morning!

"What time is it?" The other girl peered sleepily at the clock on the table between their beds.

"Just after six," she replied cheerfully, paying no attention to the low groan that greeted her announcement. "I thought I would go down and have breakfast by the pool. Want to come?" Her invitation was tossed out teasingly as she pulled on white jeans and a sunny yellow cotton shirt.

A negative grunt was her only answer.

She glanced over her shoulder, pausing in the act of tying her deck shoes. Amy's tangled dark hair and one bare shoulder was all she saw protruding from the sheets. She shrugged, undisturbed about her friend's refusal. There was no hurry, since their plane didn't leave until after lunch. She let herself quietly out of the room, tiptoeing to avoid waking the others. The muffled click from the men's bedroom drew her eyes just as she opened the outer door of the suite.

"What are you doing up?" Brandon asked, coming soft-footed across to join her.

Summer grinned, sheer good spirits lighting her eyes with a sparkle of mischief. "Creeping out to eat," she whispered in a theatrical hiss full of dire import.

Entering into the game, Brandon twirled an imaginary mustache before leering down at her. "Not without me, my beauty."

She started to giggle helplessly. He grabbed her hand and dragged her into the corridor, shutting the door softly behind them. "Are you trying to wake the sleeping chaperones?" he demanded with the right touch of fierceness.

"Who, me?" she cried, the picture of innocence.

"Then come on, woman." He tugged on her arm, hurrying her toward the elevator, which obligingly slid open at the push of the button.

That humorous beginning set the tone for the day. Summer reveled in the chance to be young, to laugh without needing a reason and to share her pleasure with someone who understood.

Before they left Paradise Island Brandon insisted on taking them all to the formal French Gardens of the Ocean Club. The beautiful white marble sculpture of Empress Josephine in the nude standing at the entrance was a well-known tourist landmark. The lovely paths bordered by lush flowering plants were a perfect setting for the fourteenth-century cloister ruins, which were brought over piece by piece from France.

It was late in the afternoon by the time they landed back on Abaco.

"Shall we try an overnighter to Freeport next?" Chuck asked as he watched his wife sink into the first chair she came to as soon as they entered their villa.

"Not a chance," she decided adamantly. "Tomorrow I'm going to find a nice soft pool lounger and spend the day lazing around."

Summer sat on the sofa closest to the wide expanse of glass overlooking the beach. As she expected, Brandon joined her.

"I guess you won't be interested in snorkeling for lobster tomorrow and cooking them on the beach," Brandon offered. "Summer says she knows just the place."

"Not for me, thanks," Chuck responded from his perch on the arm of his wife's chair. "I'm afraid lobster—whether it's Maine or Florida's clawless—makes me break out in hives. Odd, I admit, considering no other seafood bothers me, but there it is. Don't let us spoil it for you two. To be honest, I would like a quiet day myself. Amy's pool lounger sounds just right."

Brandon turned to her. "Okay with you?" he asked, a glint in his eye.

She nodded, the anticipation of being alone with him adding warmth to her gaze, turning her eyes to melting honey.

At that moment the strident ring of the phone sounded. Brandon answered it with a gesture of annoyance. "Yes, just a moment . . ." He laid the receiver on the table and rose. "I'll take it in the bedroom," he explained, a sudden businesslike tone replacing his easy manner. Even his face had changed. The smiling host was gone and a sharp-eyed businessman emerged, making Summer wonder fleetingly if she was looking at a different man.

When he shut the bedroom door behind him, she glanced at his two friends. Chuck's brow was furrowed as he hung up the phone. Obviously he knew who had called.

"Trouble?" Amy asked, voicing Summer's question.

"Maybe." His answer was flat, not denying the possibility.

It was well over two hours later before Brandon reappeared. In that time Summer had bathed and changed. She now sat alone on the villa's veranda with a tall cooler in her hand, watching the sun deepen the horizon to crimson. She heard his muffled tread behind her and turned her head.

"Shall I fix you one?" She gestured to the glass in her hand.

He nodded, coming over to sink into the chair next to hers. He was still in the same position when she returned, placing the frosty concoction at his elbow.

He looked tired, she decided, as though he were wrestling with a complicated problem. Without the devil-may-care smile she had become accustomed to, she saw the toughness, the shrewd boss Amy and Chuck knew. She sensed the ruthless drive in him, the ability to make hard decisions based on logic rather than personal preference. How she saw so much she wasn't quite certain. In fact, she was vaguely surprised at how attuned she was.

"I put a kick in it," she warned quietly when he reached for his glass.

He took a swallow and leaned back, the tension slowly easing. "That's good," he murmured, his eyes on the horizon.

Although Summer was only inches away, she was acutely aware of the distance separating them and struggled to submerge the hurt over the quick way he had withdrawn from her. She barely stifled the questions hovering on her lips. She didn't have the right to ask about his business or its problems.

Arousing from his reverie, he assuaged her curiosity. "That was my field representative in the Middle East. There's been some sort of political mix-up with the local sheik about a job we're doing over there," he explained, not taking his gaze off the setting sun.

"It sounds serious," she ventured tentatively.

He finished his cooler and turned to her, placing the empty glass on the table in front of them. "It could be, but my man out there is good, so . . ." He left the sentence unfinished as he stared at her. His eyes slowly lost the sharp, assessing gleam, darkening to a deep blue-green. "Where are our chaperones?" he asked softly.

"They went over to dinner just before you came out," she answered throatily, the tide of awareness washing over her.

He reached out his hand to brush the curls back from her ear in a curiously possessive gesture. "Why didn't you go with them? Surely you were hungry?"

There were all types of hunger—at the moment food was the least of them. "I wanted to wait for you."

"I'm glad." He sighed before leaning across to kiss her full on her waiting lips, his hand cupping the back of her neck.

When he released her, she expelled her breath in a soft gasp.

"I've been waiting all afternoon to do that," he murmured, his satisfaction plain in the dying light. "I think I could get addicted to you."

A shaft of pain unexpectedly shot through her at his teasing words. How little time they had together! Even though she knew it would end shortly, she had purposely blanked it from her mind. Now he had brought it out of hiding. For once she had no light comeback.

"What, no comment?" he grinned with the return of his former mood.

She shook her head, grateful for the darkness that hid her expression. While she hadn't left him in any doubt about the strength of her attraction, she doubted he realized she loved him. And that was one vital fact she didn't want him to know. It was her problem and she'd learn to deal with it.

When her silence lengthened, he peered at her more closely. "Maybe you are hungry at that . . . or you're falling asleep."

"No, just enjoying the silence," she said finally.

His teeth flashed white in the gloom as he grinned, rising to his feet, her hand in his. "Starvation must be setting in if you can't do better than that. I don't suppose you know a nice quiet place to eat on this cay?"

"As a matter of fact, I do."

"I like your choice," Brandon decided later as they waited for the dinner to be brought. He glanced around the small room with its tiny floral-covered tables and flickering amber candle lights.

"The food's good, too," she agreed, twisting her wineglass so that it trapped the flickering lights in its crystal bowl. "Are we still going snorkeling tomorrow?" She raised her eyes in time to see his faint start of surprise.

"Of course, unless you've decided you don't want to go?"

"No, it's not that. I thought maybe you would prefer to stay around the hotel in case there were any more calls," she explained, a glow of pleasure spreading over her at his quick response.

A thoughtful frown crossed his brow for a moment. "I don't think it's necessary. Jim should be able to handle anything that comes up," he said finally. "If not, he can always get Chuck to send someone to find us. Now, let's forget about that. I'm enjoying your company too much to spoil it with business."

Her eyebrows rose in skepticism at the glib-sounding

line and he grinned, recognizing her expression. "I mean it. Believe it or not, I rarely get a chance to relax the way I've done these last few days." His last sentence was too sincere to be doubted.

Her face cleared, although she couldn't resist baiting him a little. "That's not what I read in the papers."

He shook his head, actually looking a little hurt. "Pure window dressing in some cases, but mostly business in others. Besides, there's safety in numbers."

She stared at him, surprised by his apparent self-justification.

Fortunately the waiter arrived with their meal, eliminating any need for her response. Was he trying to explain his succession of beautiful women or was he attempting to warn her she was one of the numbers. Stealing a glance at his face as he cut into his steak, she wasn't sure. But when he lifted his eyes, trapping her gaze before she could lower her lashes, the lights glinting in their depths reassured her.

"You'd better eat," he suggested softly with a significant gesture toward her plate. "Before it gets cold."

They finished an excellent meal and were at the coffee stage when Brandon returned to their plans for the next morning.

"Have you contacted Joe about the boat?"

"No, I wasn't sure if you still wanted to go, remember?"

"Then we need to stop by the *Sea Mist* on our way back, don't we?"

She nodded. "If you still want to go by water," she agreed. "There are other places besides the cove I mentioned where we would probably have as much luck. They won't be as private, of course." She could have bitten off her tongue for adding that last comment.

Thankfully Brandon appeared to take it at face value,

merely remarking, "It will be good to escape the chatter for a while. Besides, I haven't snorkeled in so long that I don't want an audience."

Summer remembered his comment the next day as he flipped expertly over the gunwale of the anchored *Sea Mist* into the shimmering green sea. She was quick to follow him. As she bobbed to the surface and cleared her tube, he was there waiting for her, his eyes glinting with laughter through the glass of his face mask. A second later, he took her hand as they swam side by side on the surface, scanning the ocean floor for the sight of their prickly quarry.

The water was a warm liquid silk along Summer's body, clad in a brief white bikini. The heat of the sun across her back only added to the leisurely, relaxing search. Brandon's grip remained as they alternately kicked, then floated in ever increasing circles.

A gentle tug on her hand made her turn her head in his direction to find him pointing to a dark spot creeping along the sandy bottom. A small wave washed over her as he swooped down to capture the briny crustacean. Moments later he returned to her side displaying a nice-sized lobster which was irately flashing long pointed feelers in all directions.

"Two more like this?" he asked, after removing his mouthpiece and pushing his mask up.

"That should do it," she replied, following suit. "Unless you plan on feeding an army."

He laughed, a deep-throated chuckle of pure masculine satisfaction. "Nothing doing. It's taken me this long to get you alone." He glanced around the deserted cove, then back to her. "I like the place you chose for us."

She knew he was going to kiss her—here in deep water with nothing but his lean bronzed body to cling to and an angry red-brown clawless lobster flapping in one large hand.

The taste of his lips on hers held a promise of more to come. The strength of his free arm around her waist was a strong bond making her aware of every gleaming inch of his muscled frame. Of their own volition her arms curled around his neck as she pressed against him. The jar of her face mask against his effectively halted the deepening embrace. He was breathing as heavily as she when they moved apart. For a moment neither said a word, the flickering embers of desire still too volatile.

Then Brandon's lips quirked in a rueful grimace. "We had better tend to business or we won't eat today."

"Don't you mean this evening?" she teased, recovering with effort.

"Are you going to reprimand me about those calls holding us up?" he asked in turn, a look in his eye that promised retribution if she was. The phone call from his field representative in the Middle East had caught them just as they were about to leave. It had taken Brandon quite a while to handle the problem, not to mention two more calls, one to his home office and the other to the hauling firm handling the equipment delivery.

She took the precaution of kicking herself away a few feet out of reach. "I offered to postpone this trip," she called back before heading for the boat a dozen yards away.

It took most of the afternoon to find two more specimens that Brandon thought suitable for cooking. Not that Summer minded. She enjoyed the teasing intimacies as a prelude to the evening ahead of them. Although she sensed Brandon's desire matched her own, he never again allowed his control to slip.

It was late by the time they swam to shore towing the waterproof bag containing their cooking pot, eating utensils, blanket and bottle of white wine Brandon had provided—and, of course, their lobsters. Between them they quickly built the fire and prepared their fresh-caught meal. When they finished they relaxed against the warm sand couch, content just to be in each other's arms.

"Listen carefully and you can hear it hiss as it drops into the sea," he murmured against her ear as the sun touched the horizon.

It was dusk and the fire Brandon had so carefully laid to prepare their lobster glowed softly at their feet. She leaned back against his arm where it lay along the hollowed-out couch she had made in the sand and then covered with a blanket. Replete and cat-content, she lay curled against his body, her head on his shoulder, her eyes intent on the dying orange ball. As it dipped out of sight, she swore she did hear the faintest sizzle carried on the light breeze that had sprung up.

She turned, her lashes half closed in utter bliss. She stared at the clean line of his jaw, upwards to his firm lips until she settled on his eyes. Close up they were truly extraordinary: aquamarine irises flecked with gold and shielded by thick dark brown lashes. She had seen every mood reflected in their changing depths.

As she was studying him, so was he memorizing every line and curve of her slender body. The soft white cotton shirt she wore open over her bikini hid little from his gaze. The long, firm length of her, the silky, golden skin, the narrow waist and the taut proud breasts cupped in tricot.

He lifted his hand to stroke the curve above the bra, feeling the heart under his fingers speed in its rhythm. She was still beneath his touch as his exploration carried him up her slender throat to the rounded chin. His eyes fastened on her mouth and the tiny pink tip of her tongue as it moistened her lower lip.

Suddenly he could deny himself no longer. The need to taste the honeyed sweetness was too strong. He bent his head to take her lips in a devastating kiss, which seemed to Summer composed of equal parts of savagery and tenderness.

There was no thought of drawing back from his demanding mouth. She met his touch with all the pent-up desire of long abstinence and the explosive attraction she felt. She was barely aware of turning fully in his arms until they lay breast to breast together, cocooned in the bed carved by her hands.

Old as time, as elemental as their deserted paradise, the embers of desire burst into flame. No practiced lovemaking this. It was a mating of a vibrant female creature and her overwhelming virile mate.

With husky whimpers of pleasure, Summer returned his passionate embrace, parting her lips when his tongue probed for entrance. She arched her taut breasts against his chest, feeling the curly hairs penetrate the thin fabric of her suit to the sensitive peaks underneath. She trembled with each new touch of his searching, possessive hands.

When Brandon shifted momentarily, she thought he was abandoning her and cried out in protest. Seconds later she found herself lifted into his arms like a child and divested of her shirt, her bra, then her briefs. The fierce rake of his passion-hot eyes warmed her even as the breeze touched her bare skin. He laid her carefully back on their pallet before shrugging out of his suit.

With no barrier between them, Brandon lowered himself to her, his hands coming up to caress her breasts. "You're exquisite," he murmured in a raw whisper.

She felt the hardness of him against her thigh and shivered in response. His mouth captured hers, drawing her closer until the hair of his chest scraped roughly across her nipples. Tiny tremors rocked her as they stiffened with desire. She gasped aloud when he freed her lips to wrap his tongue around each rosy peak in turn. She writhed under him, held mindless in a frenzy of passion.

She ached for fulfillment, her hands dug deep into the hard muscled back, demanding completion of their union.

"Summer!" Her name was a demanding possessive rumble as he joined them in a surge of power. Power that sent shock waves of sensation to the soles of her feet. Unable even to cry out, Summer clung with all her strength to the elemental male who forged the bonds of primitive passion. Wave after wave of emotion carried them in rapid spirals to the climax of desire . . . and then it was done. An explosion so fierce they were left spent, damp and tangled together in exhaustion.

Summer lay still beneath his body, his hand still curved about her breast, the sounds of his labored breathing slowly returning to normal in her ear.

It was Brandon who broke the spell. Levering himself up on one elbow, he looked at her in the flickering firelight. There was masculine possession in his eyes as he drank in the sight of her body.

Summer gazed back at him, longing to tell him of her love. At this moment of ultimate surrender she ached to have the right.

"You're perfect, golden eyes. Did you know that?" He laid on his side facing her, his eyes never leaving her face. He curled his arm around her waist, drawing her into the curve of his body.

Summer was unable to speak, afraid she would blurt out her secret.

"Don't tell me my lovemaking has struck you dumb," he teased whimsically against her hair.

His light comment restored her voice. Her eyes

reflected her gratitude for making it easier. "No, just getting my breath back."

"No hurry, I'm enjoying the silence." His hand tucked her head under his chin. His breathing stirred the curls around her ear while his hand stroked the tousled mane in a soothing rhythm.

The heady male scent of his body, the stillness around them and the warmth of his skin against hers wrapped Summer in a cocoon of timeless contentment. She closed her eyes, savoring the feeling. "Mm, this is nice," she murmured softly.

He chuckled quietly. "Only nice?"

She poked him gently in the ribs, lifting her head to grin at him. "You know what I mean." For a long moment she stared into his face as the laughter between them gradually died.

"You're not sorry?" His low-voiced question was a serious plea, acknowledging her chaste life-style. "I wouldn't want you to be. You're very special."

Her heart contracted in momentary pain at his careful words. How wonderful it would be if he loved her. Then her lips curved in a slow, womanly smile. "No, I don't regret it."

He brought his hand up to cup her face, gazing intently into the molten honey eyes. "Will you stay with me tonight?" He saw the uncertainty flash across her face, but he made no effort to convince her. It was important to him that she choose to share his bed freely. He knew he could seduce her into a decision, but he was unaccountably reluctant to do so. He respected her spirit too much to try.

Summer was startled. While she had accepted Brandon tonight, she hadn't expected to sleep with him openly. Could she face his friends? Could she even face herself? Fool that she was, she hadn't considered the possibility. "I don't know," she whispered finally.

"You're worried about Chuck and Amy, aren't you?" he questioned, accurately summing up part of the problem. She nodded. "Don't be. Whether we're together or not would make no difference to them."

"What about me? I'm not sure I would like myself." She watched the sudden tightening of his jaw as she spoke and realized with dismay how her words sounded. She quickly placed her fingers over his lips, sealing in the angry comment she was sure was coming.

"Please hear me out," she began earnestly.

He waited silently for her to continue.

"I know this was inevitable for us; there was no way I could deny what I feel for you—but I live in this part of the world. People know me here. And while I'm not ashamed of our relationship, I can't risk my daughter's happiness, or Gussie's, for that matter. People are cruel, and you have a reputation."

"So we skulk around in the bushes like teenagers," he demanded, his temper rising. God, a simple question and she made it sound as though he had asked her to move in with him! "I'm not suggesting a permanent arrangement, damn it." He sat up, bringing her with him, then he let her go abruptly.

Summer reached for her shirt and pulled it on, suddenly chilled by the harshness in his face. She had been so certain he'd understand, but she had failed miserably.

"Besides, I don't see what the difference is between what I'm asking and how it is at the moment. Who's going to know or care if we share a bed as well as a villa?" He glared at her in frustration, seeing the telltale trembling of her fingers as she fumbled with buttoning her blouse. "Chuck and Amy certainly aren't going to discuss our living arrangements." He heard a soft, stifled sound which could have been a sob. As quickly as it had come, his anger dissipated. He reached for her, drawing her into his arms, ignoring her attempts to resist.

Summer struggled, knowing she had little chance of escaping his hold. For a second they were locked in a silent battle that left her breathless and trapped help-lessly beneath him. One leg lay across hers, pinning her to their resting place. Her arms were held above her head in a viselike grip. His face was only inches from hers.

He stared into her glittering eyes, reading the pain in their depths. He wanted to banish the shadows from the amber pools, a feeling which surprised him. He couldn't remember when he had felt the urge to protect a woman. To desire one, yes, but to keep her safe, to shield her? It was a totally new emotion for him.

"Now it's your turn to listen." He waited for her reluctant nod of agreement. He paused to gather his words. "My parents died my last year of high school, leaving me without any family—no brothers or sisters, only a law firm as guardians. There was plenty of money to do what I wanted when I wanted and no one to tell me no. I started my business mainly out of boredom with the idle rich kid's existence. It has been the only constant thing in my life. I have houses but no home. My life-style doesn't allow for permanent attach-ments. I'm a thirty-eight-year-old nomad." He chose his next words carefully. "What I'm trying to say is it's been a long time since I needed to care what someone else thought. I know how much Shannon means to you. I'll respect your judgment over what's right for her. I can't say I like it, but I will accept it."

Summer stared at him incredulously. An apology? That was it! She slowly relaxed, a reluctant amusement taking over. He looked so frustrated and irritated. She sensed his confusion, too. The sincerity of his words had been unmistakable.

"Well, say something," he demanded, impatient with her silence. She had got what she wanted, damn it. What more could he say?

"You really don't mind?" she asked, searching his face.

"What do you think? Yes, I mind! Don't you know how incredibly sexy you are? How I am supposed to sleep with you in the same house as me is the question," he retorted, torn between anger and amusement. He released her hands. "Put your arms around me."

Summer couldn't resist the husky demand any more than the mouth that suddenly captured hers. It was a soft kiss to begin with, full of tenderness and restraint, as though he sought to erase the angry words between them. She responded fully to the male need in him. How she loved the feel of his body against hers.

Pulling him closer, her lips opened like a flower beneath his. She felt his growing desire and reveled in the power she had to arouse him.

"I want you," he whispered, lifting his head for a moment to seek out the expression in her passion-darkened eyes.

Her whimper of protest at the separation answered him better than words. His fingers slid to the buttons of her shirt. In seconds he had removed the soft cloth from between them.

Having assuaged his demanding physical need earlier, he now sought to lead her into the world of sensual seduction. With the expertise of a master he brought her slowly to the peak of ecstasy, each caress, each kiss designed to give pleasure, to delight, to tantalize.

She was an exquisite lover, responding with abondon to his commands. Only when she was whimpering softly with the ache for fulfillment he had created did he cover her shimmering golden body, feeling the quivers

146

of unsatisfied passion rippling against his bare skin. She cried his name at the moment of violent yet tender union, felt him lay claim to her with a completeness she would never forget.

Much later Summer opened her eyes as Brandon stirred beside her. She blinked drowsily. "What time is it?" she asked, seeing the moonlight. She must have slept, but she didn't remember doing so.

Brandon rolled slightly away to read his watch. "Almost nine," he answered, returning to his position by her side. He nuzzled her ear, enjoying the feel of her warmth against his body.

"We'd better get our things together," she began in soft protest.

"I know." His gentle questing didn't stop.

"Brandon, the Bartos are going to be worried." She tried again. She felt him sigh as he lifted his head.

"You're right. We had better leave," he agreed, lying back and releasing her.

Summer sat up and reached for her discarded clothes. When she was dressed, she turned to find him watching her. She felt her cheeks flush under his possessive gaze. "Aren't you going to get up?"

He grinned lazily. "I don't know. Maybe I'll stay here." Seeing her worried look, he relented and got to his feet, reaching for his briefs.

It didn't take long for them to collect their gear and return it to the waterproof bag.

Brandon doused the fire last of all. "Ready?" he asked as he lifted the plastic pouch.

She nodded, taking the hand he offered. They walked barefooted to the beach and into the quiet waters of their private hideaway. They swam hand over hand, side by side to the gently bobbing white silhouette of the *Sea Mist* a few yards away.

When they reached the boat, Brandon tossed the bag he had towed on a cord from his waist over the side. For a moment they faced each other, gently treading water.

Summer ached to tell him how much their time together had meant to her, but couldn't without betraying her love. She could only gaze at him, the longing locked inside of her.

In response to her plea, he pulled her close for a moment as though he, too, was reluctant to leave their haven. The embrace was short but fierce. She watched as he heaved himself into the boat, then leaned over to give her a hand. "I'll get the anchor after I stow this," he said when she stood dripping beside him.

She nodded, picking up one of the towels she had left on a deck chair in preparation for their return swim. She rubbed herself dry as she headed for the controls.

A short time later the engines rumbled to life. On bow, Brandon brought the anchor line in. She waited until she heard the thud of the heavy weight against the deck before easing the throttle forward.

He joined her in the cockpit as she pointed the *Sea Mist* toward open water.

There was something of an other-worldly magic in piloting a boat across a deserted stretch of ocean in the moonlight, Summer decided as she slipped into bed later that night. Guided by a tiny needle in a crimson illuminated compass, she had given the *Sea Mist* its head to follow the silver lunar path stretching a seemingly endless trail before them. Though they spoke little on their homeward journey, she had scarcely noticed. In fact, the silence had been in keeping with the unreal sensation. She fell asleep, a smile on her lips, remembering the final kiss outside her bedroom door.

It had said so much of the man she was coming to know. It held all the desire she felt, yet not once did he try to change her mind. She loved him all the more for his restraint.

She awoke the next morning to the sounds of voices and doors closing. A quick glance at her clock showed it was too early for anyone to be up. In fact, it was barely light. She slid out of bed and reached for her robe.

Brandon's bedroom door ajar was the first thing she saw as she entered the hall. Her initial thought was that someone was ill. Seeing the downstairs lights on she was convinced of it. Was it Amy? she wondered, catching the sound of Chuck's voice when she crossed to the open doorway. Brandon was on the phone, a pair of slacks covering his otherwise bare body. They had obviously been pulled on in a hurry, for the belt hung unbuckled. Chuck was busy at the foot of the bed with an empty suitcase and a stack of clothes.

Brandon looked up to where she stood frozen in place. The angry sparks in his eyes told of a temper just barely held in check. Deep lines cut into the bronze skin around his nose and mouth, making him appear the high-powered businessman he was. What had happened?

"Right, an hour . . . no, just one passenger . . . when will we land?" His questions were a staccato bark to whoever was on the other end of the line. He hung up the phone with a hurried bang.

"Pack those for me so Chuck can dress to take me to the airport," he commanded, striding past her on the way to the bathroom. "I need a shower." He glanced toward his friend. "We only have an hour, so hurry up. I'll brief you on the way."

Chuck nodded, pausing just long enough to thank Summer as she took over folding and packing. Her hands were quick, but even so Brandon was back fully dressed before she had finished. He snapped the lid shut the moment her fingers were clear. "I must go," he announced, case in hand, already moving toward the door.

Summer trailed behind, her mind a tangled mass of questions. "Where?" she asked, settling for the most obvious.

"The Mideast project," he replied over his shoulder with an irritated snap. "God, what a mess!"

Seconds later she stood facing Amy, the closed door muffling the sounds of the rented car's engine.

Amy looked as stunned as she felt. "Do you have any idea what happened?"

"No, I was hoping you did," Summer admitted, feeling slightly better knowing Amy was equally uninformed.

"I've never seen Brandon so worked up," Amy observed in amazement. "He didn't even take time to say goodbye."

8

Amy's words remained to echo over and over in Summer's mind, giving her no peace by night or day. One phone call, that's all, since Brandon had raced into the predawn darkness without a word to her in explanation. There had been no message for her when he had called Chuck later that same day en route to the Middle East. Maybe if she had been at the villa that first afternoon, Brandon might have . . .

She shook her head impatiently, slapping the charts she should have been studying for their return trip to Jupiter against the *Sea Mist*'s console.

What have I done? she cried out in her heart. Five days. Five whole days! Did she mean so little that he had erased what they shared from his mind? She raked her hand through her windblown curls, her face showing her hurt and bewilderment. Chuck and Amy had decided to take a driving tour of the island before they left the next day. She had been invited, but she couldn't bring herself to face any more of Amy's lighthearted enjoyment. Everyone but Brandon wanted her. Even

Joe tried to convince her to join him at Salty's for a while. She winced mentally, remembering the understanding in his eyes when she had refused.

Was she so transparent? She hoped not. She had tried to conceal her feelings the past few days as she had once again taken the Bartos out to the fishing grounds. After all, it was only her mind and heart that carried the special significance of the night on the beach when she had given her love.

To anyone else she was just another woman to succumb to Brandon's charm and expertise. One more in a line. Even now he could be choosing a replacement. Or had one. Agony darkened her eyes as she stared across the crowded marina.

For five years she had shared her life with no man. She knew when she gave herself to Brandon she was going to pay for each second of pleasure. And she was. Every breath she drew was torture, every empty nighttime hour a black void filled with unappeased desire. She ached for the feel of him, the touch of him, the scent of him and, most of all, the sight of him. Never having known passion, never having felt the driving need for a man, she now found her unchained senses a constant torment. It showed in her eyes, the forced smile she wore and the tension in her slender body.

"You done, Summer girl?"

Joe's soft query startled her. She glanced over her shoulder, the shadow of his broad frame shutting out much of the light in the small cabin. She didn't have enough warning to cover her expression, and Joe's indrawn hiss told her that he had seen.

"No, I'm not," she answered quietly, turning back to the roll in front of her. It cracked as she unfurled it.

Joe cleared his throat, the sound bringing Summer's gaze to his face. He sat down in the chair at her side.

Reading the uncertainty in his faded eyes, she watched the awkward shift of his feet.

"I'm here, you know . . . if you need me," he offered gruffly. "I don't gossip . . ."

She nodded, more touched than she could put into words. Some of the pain locked inside her eased. She smiled, a slow curve of her lips. "Thanks, Joe. I'll remember."

He reached for the chart under her elbow. "Going back the same way?"

"Yes, it's the quickest," she agreed, knowing he accepted and understood her need for privacy.

"Good. I've been missing Gussie's tongue. Besides, I bet that blond doll of yours has grown a foot."

At the mention of Shannon, Summer grinned, momentarily forgetting her heavy heart. "You know, that little imp called me at three this morning to tell me the tooth fairy left her two dollars!"

Joe chuckled. "She didn't. Where was Gus?"

"She was supposed to be sleeping, Shannon said," she replied, recalling her daughter's gleeful laughter at having caught her aunt in the act of exchanging her tooth for two new green bills. "I'm afraid Shannon's discovered the secret of the tooth fairy. It would be wonderful to be young again—seeing the world opening before your eyes . . ." She paused, her voice altering to a bitter note Joe had never heard before. "It's too bad we can't stay children forever. It's a lot less painful."

"Sure it is, girl, but not nearly as challenging. For every rotten thing that happens there's plenty of good, and you know it," he scolded her.

Her eyes were sad as she stared at him. "Yes, I suppose I do," she agreed.

There was silence between them for a moment

before Summer retrieved her chart and rerolled it. "I'm going back to the villa." She got up, stretching slightly.

Joe rose, his bulk making the close confines of the cabin area even smaller. "I'll have 'er ready for you at daybreak," he offered, referring to the outfitting of the *Sea Mist* for the run back. There were gas tanks to top off, coolers to ice, water containers to fill and the dockmaster to see. "You're coming down with the Bartos?"

"Might as well if you're going to take over and do my work for me." Her return to their usual teasing manner, strained though it was, visibly relieved Joe.

A few minutes later he watched her stride down the path. There wasn't a hint of the pain he had witnessed earlier in the lithe, free-swinging walk so curiously her own. His weathered face wore a heavy frown. He knew that man wanted her, but God help him, he had not believed Summer would be duped by his slick city ways. Not that he didn't like the man, but he sure wasn't right for Summer.

"Damned fool playboy," he mumbled under his breath. "Got no respect for a decent woman." He glared across to the now empty path as though he expected to see the subject of his anger walk down it. "He shoulda known she'd take it hard. The least he coulda done was let 'er down easy."

The next morning Summer awoke early in her darkened room. While she waited for the telltale gray of the approaching dawn, she forced herself to examine her feelings. She didn't like what she saw.

Sure she had been hurt; she was still hurting and probably would for a while to come. But nothing lasted forever. She had seen enough pain in her life to realize that. The trick was surviving until the unbearable was bearable. When Tom had died there had been three-year-old Shannon and Tom's Rest to occupy her time. Well, this wasn't much different.

Brandon was gone. She had to accept and learn to live with it. The story about a business crisis was less believable with each passing day. If it was a serious problem surely Chuck would have mentioned something. Instead, she had heard nothing about what was going on. There wasn't anything in the newspaper either—she knew because she had checked.

So that left only one conclusion. Brandon had been called away, all right. Once clear of her, with time to think, he must have realized her surrender created more of a problem than he wanted to handle. So he took the easy way out. He let their short-lived affair die. It wasn't a pretty picture, but it wasn't a new one, either.

It was too late to wish she hadn't believed there was a different man under the newspaper image. That Brandon—her lover—only existed in her dreams. Tears she rarely shed trickled down her cheeks as she lay in aching stillness in the dimly lit room. She didn't cry out, the pain was too deep. She felt mortally wounded by his apparent betrayal, and the tiny crystal drops of her broken heart fell unheeded on the snow-white pillowcase.

More than an hour later, she heard sounds of Chuck and Amy stirring. Dressed in her usual garb of jeans and tee-shirt, her face cleared of her emotional soulsearching, she lifted her packed duffel from her bed and entered the hall.

Amy came out of her bedroom almost simultaneously. "Hi, did you sleep well?"

Summer's mask was in place and she smiled almost naturally. "Fine," she answered. "Are you two about ready?"

"Chuck's just finishing up now. I thought I would put the coffee on."

"Good idea. I could use a cup," Summer agreed.

They all ended up on the terrace, coffee mugs in hand.

"It's going to be a shame to go home after this. If it weren't for the boys, I wouldn't go back," Amy admitted with a rueful grin. She glanced at her carefully tanned arms and golden legs in satisfaction. "I'm going to be the envy of my friends."

Her husband chuckled. "We still have a week left, don't forget. We're under orders to make the most of it."

"Since when?" Amy asked in surprise. "I know we have seven days, but that's the first I've heard about anything else."

"I talked to Brandon last night," Chuck announced casually, refilling his cup from the percolator on the table at his elbow. He missed his audience's reaction.

Summer, sitting on his right, the table between them, paused in the act of raising her cup to her lips.

"Did he call here?" his wife demanded, unknowingly voicing Summer's own question.

"No, I contacted him." Chuck leaned back in his chair, his head turned to his wife on his left. "It took me three tries to find him. I swear the kind of life he leads would kill me. Finally reached him at some party."

Summer carried her mug the rest of the way to her mouth. So she had been right all along. The crisis, whatever it was, was over. Brandon was again on the move.

"Is he coming back to Florida?" Amy asked.

"He doesn't think so. I told him I would keep an eye on the boat repairs for him."

"I'm surprised he remembered the *Shalimar* with everything else that's going on," his wife observed, rising to collect the dishes.

Up until now Summer had been a silent spectator.

156

"Mr. Marshall doesn't strike me as the type to forget things important to him," she commented. She was appalled at the bitterness of her words.

Apparently neither of her listeners heard anything unusual. Chuck was already nodding his head in agreement. "You're so right. Brandon only forgets what he wants to. He amazes me. His mind can be on one vital topic, yet he rarely loses his grip on the smaller issues that exist at the same time. I suppose his uncanny ability to juggle so many things at once is the basis for his success. That and his ruthless determination to reach a goal."

Every word Chuck uttered was another stake in Summer's heart. Thank heaven she would be free of the Bartos and the constant reminder of Brandon Marshall in a few more hours. The sooner she could return to her simple life the better. She desperately needed the sanity of her real existence to regain her emotional balance.

It seemed Joe was equally eager to get back. The *Sea Mist* engines were purring softly, already warmed, when Summer and her passengers stepped on board.

Once free of the marina area Summer eased the throttle forward to maximum cruising speed. The craft responded beautifully, perhaps sensing its owner's urgency. This time there was no companionable conversation to while away the hours of unrelenting miles of open sea. Summer kept her eyes glued to the beckoning horizon, leaving Joe to deal with their guests. She had one thought. Get home. Back to the safe routine that had been her salvation in the past.

It was only when she stood watching the Bartos' rental car disappear down the road that she realized how tense she was. Usually being on the *Sea Mist* relaxed her no matter what her problems. This time she felt as though every muscle was drawn tight, each nerve

157

raw with pain from memory. She sighed deeply and turned wearily toward The Nest.

"Mom, hey, Mom!"

Summer glanced up when she heard her daughter's voice. She stood unmoving as Shannon, bright blond curls dancing with sunlight, flashed down the dirt track that led to the inlet's park. A slow smile temporarily erased the shadows from her eyes. There was pride, too. Shannon was a special gift. A sunny child full of an adventuring spirit. As she got closer, Summer could see the splashes of sea water on the once crisp navy shorts, not to mention the sand crusting on her slender brown legs.

Her daughter hurled herself into her mother's waiting arms. Her golden blond baby-fine hair mingled with Summer's sun-streaked tawny mane as Shannon hugged her neck. She leaned back to stare at her.

"I was on the jetty. I waved, but you didn't see me. Boy, I've missed you. Gussie baked a Mississippi-mud cake just for us to celebrate," she announced, naming her favorite dessert—a pitch-black chocolate and sour cream cake served warm from the oven and iced with gooey midnight frosting. "We've even got lemonade to go with it."

"Whoa, imp," Summer teased, her arms tightening around her daughter's petite form. "Have you been storing all your words until I got back?"

"No, silly," Shannon grinned. She wiggled her legs impatiently. "You can let me down now." She glanced over her shoulder to the trees bordering the parking area.

Summer's gaze picked out the unruly red hair of Shannon's boyfriend of the moment as he headed for his parent's trailer farther down the beach. A fleeting shadow crossed her face. How quickly they learn. "I'm glad you took Eric with you. You did tell Gus where you were going, didn't you?" she asked, eyeing her daughter after she had let her down.

She nodded. "I know. Don't go near the rocks unless the tide is out. Don't go to the park alone. Always tell you or auntie where I'm going. No swimming unless there is an adult with me." Shannon dutifully ticked off the safety rules one by one on each tiny finger. "Oh, yes, and one more. Don't talk to strangers . . . especially men."

"Good girl," her mother approved, wishing she had followed that rule herself. Banishing her thoughts with determination, she held out her hand and felt Shannon's sandy fingers grab hers. "Come on, I'll race you to the mud cake."

Her daughter giggled. "Not unless I get a head start."

"You're on," Summer agreed, releasing her grip. "I'll give you to the count of ten." She bent over in an exaggerated runner's crouch. "Ready . . . set . . . go!" She started counting, her eyes on the racing figure. It was so good to be home again. Nightly phone calls were no substitute for your own child, she thought as she sprinted toward The Nest.

It was a tie. Mother and daughter spilled into the hallway just as Gussie came down the last step of the spiral staircase from the upper deck.

"I could hear you two comin' a mile away," she scolded them, surveying the flushed faces of her two dearest relatives. "It was a good trip, I see, although I'm not sure I like that darker tan."

Summer glanced at her daughter, evading Gussie's all-seeing eyes as she agreed. "Yes, it went very well." She pointed to the bathroom. "Go get cleaned up, imp."

Gussie's smile faded slightly as she caught the odd note in Summer's voice. Yet when Summer looked up, she could find nothing unusual in her expression.

"Something wrong?"

Gussie shook her head, uneasy but not sure why. "No, nothing."

She was to remember her vague feeling more and more as the days passed. On the surface everything went on as before. Business was booming, the charters booked solid, yet something was not right. She couldn't put her finger on just what was out of sync, but she knew somehow Summer had changed.

Summer was aware of Gussie's disquiet, and she tried her best to act as normal as possible. She forced herself to eat even when the thought of food threatened to choke her. She smiled and made herself sleep simply by working her body into exhaustion. But no matter what she did, she knew her sister-in-law wasn't fooled.

It had been a full week today since she had returned. There was no way she could go on denying anything was wrong. She knew that this morning when Gussie caught her emptying her breakfast into the dog's food bowl. Only Shannon's timely entrance saved her from a cross-examination then.

In a few minutes she had to go out on the terrace and face Gussie's questions. She had lingered as long as she dared over the dishes. She knew if she tried to go to bed early Gussie would only be waiting for her in the morning.

She wiped the last pot dry, put it away, then hung the towel on its hook, each movement slow and precise. Mentally she braced herself for the ordeal she knew was to come. Her love for Gussie as well as the care she had been given over the years made it impossible for Summer to deny her the right to her questions. In a way she almost welcomed them. Maybe she needed to talk.

Gussie was waiting patiently just as Summer knew she would be.

Summer took her usual place and propped her feet on the railing. Seconds ticked by in silence. Then Summer gathered herself to begin. "I fell in love, Gus," she announced in an unemotional tone, taking the wind out of the older woman's sails. "But not blindly. I knew what I was doing . . . or thought I did." She picked up her coffee mug and sipped slowly.

Gussie's eyes were trained on her seemingly calm profile. She was amazed at her control, because obviously something had gone seriously wrong. She remained silent, knowing from experience Summer would tell her only as much as she intended.

"I knew Brandon wasn't in love with me—knew he didn't want anything permanent." She turned to stare into Gussie's sympathetic face. "But it didn't matter. I decided to take the little time we had together." She glanced away back over the darkened inlet. "I lost that too. One night, that's all we had, then he left. He didn't even say goodbye." All of Summer's pent-up emotion came through her last low-voiced words, a telling epitaph for a love affair.

Gussie gasped softly as the full significance hit her. "You mean he gave you no reason at all. Surely Joe said something to me about his being called away on business."

"He was and at first I believed it. Oh, I was hurt when he left so quickly without a word to me, but I understood—or thought I did. When he called Chuck later that day, I tried to remember how serious his problems were, and how worried he was bound to be. I understood when he didn't ask to speak to me, but there's a limit to how many excuses you can think up.

Chuck tried to reach him before we left. He finally got him at a party, not business at all," Summer concluded.

Gussie wore a thoughtful expression. "Don't you think you are being unrealistic?" She held up her hand when Summer started to interrupt. "No, wait. Isn't it possible Brandon was still working? You don't know for sure he wasn't. And as far as his not saying anything to you . . . how could he? You two weren't alone, were you? You didn't want him to send you a message through his friend?"

"Don't you think I haven't said all of this to myself? The fact remains he's been gone almost two weeks. Surely in that time he had a moment to phone or write. There simply isn't any plausible reason for his continued silence except that he is regretting our affair. And he's taking this way to end it."

"It was what you expected, or so you say."

Summer nodded, unable to deny the truth of her assessment. "I did, but not like this." She paused, inhaling sharply. "I was a convenience, the available woman. He didn't want the blonde anymore, so he chose something new—me." Her voice broke on a note of despair. "I never was a person at all, don't you see?" she finished in a dead whisper.

Gussie's eyes filled with tears. She ached to hold out her arms to comfort Summer in her agony. She understood now. Not only had she lost the man she loved, but her pride in herself as a woman had been cruelly stripped away as well. There was not one word she could say to ease that hurt and she knew it.

Gussie studied her tightly controlled expression in the softly lit darkness. Although her eyes glistened betrayingly, there wasn't a tear in sight. It had been that way when Tom died, too, she remembered. All the grief was locked inside then and it was now.

"I wish I could turn back the clock for you, child," she offered in heartfelt sympathy. "I truly wanted you to love a man passionately, but never like this. With you being you, I honestly meant marriage. I wish now I had never opened my mouth."

9

~~~~~~~~~~~~~~~~

"I'm sorry about the delay, Mr. Marshall. The company sent the wrong part and we only got this one yesterday."

Brandon surveyed his boat with resignation. In its cradle, free of its natural element, it appeared twice as big as it was yet lost none of its graceful beauty. "How long before it will be finished?"

"Wednesday at the latest." The marina owner spread his hands apologetically.

Brandon nodded. He didn't mind the holdup anyway, since the *Shalimar* was only one of the reasons he had returned to Florida. His eyes drifted east along the beach to Tom's Rest. He saw the familiar lines of the *Sea Mist* still at her slip.

"Hey, Dad! Can we fish off the short dock?"

Brandon turned his head, catching sight of a group of shorts-clad girls coming across the asphalt yard. The bright blond head of the child beside the leader of the small horde caught his eye. He recognized Shannon McAllister about the same time she saw him.

"Mr. Marshall, hi." The child drew slightly away from

164

her friends to address him. "When did you get back? Did you come to see about your boat?"

His lips twitched at her quick succession of questions. "I did, but it's not ready yet. What are you doing here?"

"Jenny," she pointed to the dark-haired little girl talking earnestly with her father, "is having a sleep-over for her birthday. We just finished breakfast and now we're going to fish if her dad says it's okay."

"A sleep-over?" His brow quirked inquiringly at the odd term.

Shannon grinned. "Well, we didn't do much sleeping."

Brandon chuckled in amusement at her admission. "So what did you do?" he asked curiously, finding he really wanted to know.

Shannon shrugged, "Played records, told ghost stories, ate cake, you know." She glanced down toward her house for a moment. "I guess Mom isn't going out."

He followed her eyes. "Maybe her charter cancelled," he suggested.

"Nope, Mom doesn't take anyone out on Sunday. That's our day. 'Cept today we're going to have it in the afternoon. I told her I'd come home early, but she said no." She paused to study him seriously. "You don't suppose she's feeling bad cause I'm not there, do you? Maybe I ought to go back; then we can take the boat out."

Brandon gazed into the vividly blue eyes and the worried expression. She was her mother's child, with Summer's deep capacity for emotion. As once before, he went down on one knee, uncaring of soiling his pants. "How about it if I go see your mother in your place. We could even take the *Sea Mist* out. Would you stay and enjoy your party then?"

Shannon tipped her head to one side as though weighing his offer.

"Your mother's not going to feel very nice if she thinks she spoiled your fun, you know," he suggested quietly.

"Okay, but only if you promise."

"I promise," he vowed, holding out his hand to seal their pact.

Shannon placed her fingers in his confidently.

Summer came out of The Nest, pausing only long enough to slide on her sunglasses. She had taken to wearing them more often to cover the darkening shadows under her eyes. She had lost weight, too. Her clothes hung on her slender frame. The work she purposely did to help her sleep at night took its toll. Even her exhausted slumber was haunted by Brandon's specter. He was a dream lover with an insatiable appetite. She should hate him, but she didn't. Even though she tried to wipe him from her heart, his memory still lingered.

She stepped onto the quiet beach and headed for the dock. Today was Sunday, the one day in the week when she didn't take charters. Although the bait store was already going full swing, the slips were practically empty, with most of the commercial boats having left at dawn. The few people milling around the remaining craft were mostly sightseeing customers. She walked slowly down the planking, her eyes downcast. She was glad she had this time alone. Shannon was off to an overnight birthday party and Joe had gone with one of his commercial fishing buddies to net the Spanish mackerel schooling just off the beach. So that left only her and the *Sea Mist*.

"Hello, Summer."

She stopped abruptly and glanced up. Less than a foot away stood the embodiment of her dreams. Lean, tan, dark sable hair falling over his brow, Brandon was braced against the *Sea Mist*'s cabin, his arms folded across his chest. He looked perfectly relaxed and completely at home.

"Where did you come from?" she demanded. It wasn't the smartest of openings, but it was the best she could do at the moment.

Brandon pushed lazily upright, dropping his hands. "I saw Shannon while I was checking on the *Shalimar*. She said you were going out alone today," he explained, ignoring her question.

"I am," she returned coldly. "Completely alone." The emphasis on the last word was unmistakable.

He eyed her taut figure. "I'm afraid not," he replied slowly. "I made a promise to a cute little eight-year-old."

"Shannon?" she questioned sharply. "What did she tell you?" Suspicion crept into her voice, and she saw his expression change as he heard it. An intent look replaced his casual air. He was watching her closely now.

"Only that she was worried you might be lonely. She was thinking of coming home early to keep you company until I offered to go in her place."

"Why?"

"Because I want to talk to you."

She stared at him, struck by the determined note in his statement. "Well, I don't want to talk to you," she stated, moving toward the bow line. The sooner she escaped his presence the better. She was terrified he would guess how glad she was to see him. So far the sheer surprise of his appearance had worked for her. But she was still far too vulnerable to resist his appeal for much longer.

She bent over, deftly undoing the rope. Thank goodness she had warmed the *Sea Mist*'s engines up before breakfast. At least she didn't need to wait to make her escape. As she straightened, she saw he had released the stern line.

"You go ahead and start her up. I'll hold the lines until you're ready," he offered before she could speak.

She nodded, striving to keep her surprise and relief of his easy acceptance of her departure from showing on her face. She stepped across the deck to mount the ladder to the flybridge. Seconds later the motors purred to life. She eased the throttle to idle, at the same time shouting for him to cast off. The boat was already moving away from the dock when she heard a distinct thud and the *Sea Mist* rocked slightly. She glanced over her shoulder to see Brandon in the cockpit. She glared through the tinted screen of her glasses. Damn that man, she swore silently. For a moment she debated returning to the slip, then her anger got the better of her. So he wanted to talk, did he.

"May I come up?" He stood balanced midway up the ladder.

"I can't stop you," she replied coldly. "But whatever you're planning to do, hurry up and do it."

He ignored her last comment, merely ascending the rest of the way and taking his place on the small bench she occupied.

Summer scanned the mouth of the inlet. It was clear; no boats clogging its narrow mouth. Her hand tightened on the throttle as she pushed it forward.

The *Sea Mist* responded with a low growl and a surge of speed. The nose came up as the boat leapt out of the water, a wide foaming wake streaming behind.

Beside her, Summer felt Brandon's surprise. She headed straight out, ignoring the safer south channel. Since it was high tide and calm as a mill pond, she knew there was no danger. She half expected her passenger to make some comment. He didn't. She could see the boats of the weekend anglers grouped together to the right, so she swung north toward the open sea. The way she felt right now, she wanted plenty of room. When she finally slowed to a stop and cut the engines she had her wish. The other craft were only tiny specks on the horizon, the coastline marked by a ragged line of condominiums. The water here was a deep, dark blue, indicating the *Sea Mist* was adrift in the Gulf Stream.

Although Brandon had ridden in silence, Summer was conscious of his waiting patience. It seemed to her there was no anger in it, only a determination to talk to her.

Summer turned, finding his eyes on her, an unreadable expression in their depths. She resolutely kept her mouth closed. She had decided to let him speak first. He seemed in no hurry to begin. Finally, just when she thought her good intentions wouldn't survive another second, he broke the silence.

"You've lost weight," he observed slowly. "Why?"

She glared at him, thankful she had her sunglasses on. Leave it to him to make a comment on her appearance first thing after not seeing her for weeks. "Working," she replied curtly. "It's the tourist season, remember."

His brow raised in disbelief. "Is that the only reason?"

She was quick to snap at his challenge. "What else?"

"Missing me, maybe." His eyes were fixed on hers, shielded by their silvered screen. He reached for her glasses, whipping them off in one smooth motion. "That's better," he murmured in satisfaction as he calmly put them in his breast pocket.

Summer's eyes blazed. She grabbed for her property only to have her hand caught and held. "You have no right—" she began furiously.

"I have all the rights I need," he replied grimly, his own temper rising. "I want to see your face when I say what I have to say." He raked an impatient hand

169

through his hair. "I've come halfway around the world to get to you, woman. The least you could do is show a little enthusiasm. I've had better receptions than this from my enemies."

"What did you expect?" she snapped, tugging ineffectually to free her captured hand. "An open-armed hero's welcome?"

He drew back as though slapped. His jaw clenched. "No, I thought you might be glad to see me."

"Why?" she demanded. "Because we slept together? You should know the rules better than I. A little thing like a nocturnal romp doesn't entitle either party to a blasted thing." She knew she had hit home with that jibe. A surge of red darkened his tan; his eyes were twin points of steel impaling her.

"Listen, you sharp-tongued cat. I'm not claiming anything . . . yet. At the moment I'm not even sure what I'm doing here," he growled, releasing his hold on her fingers only long enough to grab her shoulders. He tightened his grip as she strained backwards.

His hands bit into her skin as she tried to pry his fingers away. "Let go of me . . . you . . . you . . ." she shouted, stammering in her rage. She overbalanced when he released her abruptly. Only his quick reflexes saved her as he pulled her back in place.

Brandon glanced around. "Look, let's go below. I haven't worked nearly three solid weeks trying to appease a petty tyrant to release my men and my equipment just so we can shout at each other."

"Work? Is that what you call it?" She could just guess what sex his so-called tyrant was. She was appalled at the bitterness of her own question. Until this moment she had not fully realized how much the possibility of a rival bothered her.

He shook his head, not answering. "Below." He

emphasized his one-word command with a gesture toward the lower deck.

Knowing it was useless to argue since he was completely capable of bodily removing her from her perch, she descended the ladder, following him to the short padded bench in the cabin.

When she was seated beside him he didn't give her a chance to speak. "What exactly to you think I've been doing?" he asked, beginning to realize something about her anger was all out of proportion. There was no denying he hadn't contacted her, but that wouldn't account for her attitude.

"You tell me." She gazed back at him, unyielding.

"What did Chuck tell you?"

Her reply was uncompromising. "Nothing. The same as you did." She jumped as a sharp oath rent the air.

"You mean all this time you didn't know what was going on? I thought Chuck would keep you informed. It never occurred to me he would keep the situation confidential," he explained, beginning to have some idea of what she must have believed. He was well aware of his playboy public image. It was a decided advantage in negotiations from his point of view because it frequently led his opponents to underestimate him.

She nodded slowly, a faint hope beginning to stir at his words. His anger at her accusations, his shock at her remark about a hero's welcome pointed to something . . . but what?

Without a word he wrapped his arms around her and drew her close. This time she didn't resist. His heart throbbed under her ear as he held her for a moment. "I didn't desert you, golden eyes," he murmured against her hair.

She relaxed slightly, desperately wanting to believe him. "You didn't?" she questioned in a soft whisper, half afraid to ask. She felt him sigh, then release her.

"I admit I didn't try to contact you, but I didn't cut and run as you obviously thought."

She searched his face; his eyes met and held hers with unflinching directness. She believed him.

"You're not going to ask me where I've been, what I've been doing?" he asked when she didn't speak.

"I'd like to know," she admitted frankly, "but no, I'm not going to demand an explanation."

"You trust me that much?" The amazement he felt was clearly reflected in his voice. His hand came up to gently touch the side of her face, a look of wonder in his eyes.

She rubbed her cheek along his palm in a feline gesture of agreement. "Yes."

For a long moment they remained immobile; then he took his hand away.

"You knew Jim was having trouble with the sheik who owned the land around the building site? I told you a little about the problem after the first call."

She nodded silently.

"Well, it seems the old boy wasn't satisfied with the money we were paying him for the right of way across his property. He figured a big American concern had dollars to burn. So he tripled the price. When we didn't pay, he decided to hold up the whole job by denying us access. That was the second call." His voice hardened. "His tactics didn't work. We had a contract not only with him but also with the construction company. Every delay was costing us money and time. Without our machines, they couldn't even begin."

Summer could imagine his anger. There was a ruthless cast to his features as he paused before continuing.

"Under my orders, the men proceeded across his land. They were nearly there when they were attacked." He ignored her gasp of surprise. "No one was killed, thank God. The third phone call, the morning I left, was to tell me he was holding the men and the machines for ransom."

"No wonder you raced away," she murmured. "Why didn't you say something then?"

He shrugged. "At the time all I could think about were those twenty people. They were handpicked for the job, most of them had families. I couldn't forget I had given the orders to push ahead."

"Did the sheik release them?" she asked, understanding now some of the pressure he had been under.

"Finally, after keeping us on tenterhooks for nearly two weeks," he admitted. "Most of the time he pretended everything was perfectly normal. He even had the gall to give a party in my honor. Chuck called that night—maybe he told you." He glanced at her inquiringly.

Her expression told him what conclusions she had drawn without her saying a word.

"Damn, not that, too."

She nodded, a smile beginning to form at his groan of exasperation.

"It's a wonder you didn't push me off the dock."

"Don't think the thought didn't cross my mind," she teased, her heart feeling pounds lighter now that she realized he hadn't intentionally deserted her. He still hadn't fully explained why she had not heard from him, but that fact seemed to be losing its importance. He was here.

As though she had spoken her thoughts aloud, he continued, his voice even, giving nothing away. "That still doesn't tell you everything, does it?"

She shook her head, mentally bracing herself for what was to come.

"That night on the beach—here he hesitated almost as though he were groping for the right words—was

173

special. There was something between us . . ." He gestured helplessly. "I think you felt it, too."

"I did," she agreed quietly. So he had been touched by the same magic. She studied him, seeing the uncharacteristic uncertainty in his eyes.

"It threw me." He stared at her, willing her to understand. "I'm thirty-eight. I've lived too many years on my own to suddenly come up against a woman like you and cope. At first I was intrigued by your beauty and your unusual—to say the least—occupation." He saw her astounded look and grinned slightly. "You're a beautiful woman, you know. There was Joyce, of course, and no matter what my reputation, I don't bed women like most people chain-smoke. When she left I was relieved. Originally she invited herself. As it turned out it was a farewell voyage for us both. Our affair, such as it was, had died a long time ago."

He paused, his hand going to cover hers where it lay on the seat between them.

"I wanted to get to know you better and, I admit, make love to you. Yet the more we were together the more interested I became in you. That's never happened to me before."

She could well imagine. After all, a man didn't need to know much about the type of women he escorted except how to please them.

"Jim's call gave me a perfect excuse for backing off. I could have called, but I needed time to come to terms with what was happening to me. You're a potent mixture, golden eyes." His teasing didn't hide his earnestness.

"And did you?" she asked, her lashes dropping. She dared not believe the tender note she heard in his own special endearment.

His other hand lifted her chin until she opened her eyes to meet his aquamarine gaze. "No, I'm afraid

174

not." He came closer, his movement slow, almost tentative, until his lips were only inches away. "I'm not sure I want to, either," he whispered, his breath warm against her skin.

Summer wasn't certain which of them moved, but suddenly his arms wrapped around her, drawing her that last space needed to reach his lips. The explosion of long pent-up desire was as inevitable as the tide. Mindlessly, she clung to the strong body of the man she loved. He was the source of her strength and her weakness.

When finally he drew back slightly, allowing her to catch her breath, she lay pliant, softly gasping in his arms.

"Come with me, Summer with the golden eyes. Share my life. See the world by my side." His voice, husky with desire, matched the sea-green flame of his gaze.

Through the heat steadily rising within her she heard his words. Tiny snowflakes fell one by one as each syllable trickled through her mind. Where was the love, the commitment?

"To live with you?" she asked, her voice so calm she was sure someone else had said those deadly words.

He nodded, not catching the full significance of her question. He did feel her withdrawal. His brow creased in puzzlement when she withdrew from his arms.

"I can't." Her answer was flat, without inflection. The pain was so intense she felt she would shatter if she let so much as a hint of emotion break through.

"What do you mean, you can't?" he demanded incredulously. "If it's the other women, forget them. I've never asked anyone but you to share my life. I've never wanted to."

She shook her head slowly. She had to make him understand. "I can't handle your kind of relationship. I can't give Shannon that type of image of her mother, either."

"What the hell is that supposed to mean?" he questioned, beginning to get angry.

"What happens when you're tired of me?" She answered his question with one of her own.

"Who says I'll get tired of you?"

There was understanding and deep sadness in the honey pools that gazed into his grim face. "I love you, Brandon, probably more than I'll ever love any man, but I won't be your mistress." Somehow she felt no fear in admitting her love. She wasn't ashamed of how she felt. She suspected he knew anyway. "I believe in marriage, in a home, in children. I can't live the way you are offering me."

He stared at her in disbelief. She loved him, but she didn't want him.

"If it's Shannon, I'll hire a tutor for her. She can travel with us. Think of the fun and education she would get out of it," he found himself almost pleading.

"No."

He grabbed her shoulders, frustrated by her refusal to even consider it.

"Why?"

"I told you," she explained patiently.

He stared at her, the realization that she meant every word slowly sinking in. His hands dropped and his face assumed a masklike blankness. "That's it, then." There was defeat in his voice.

Summer rose, leaving him sitting there, and headed for the controls. It was time to go home. She needed to escape his presence. How often she had felt this way in the past few weeks. When he was away she ached for him, when he was near she sought a refuge. It would be funny if it weren't so tragic. She didn't dare think about what she had just sacrificed. It would be so easy to turn around and take it all back, to let him hold her, to forget the values she had been brought up believing. But what about tomorrow? The day when the magic wore off? When a new girl took her place? What then?

The trip back seemed unending, the silence between them more tense than when they had come out.

"Will you have dinner with me tonight?" he asked as he joined her on the dock after securing the stern line.

She stared at him, speechless at the polite request. "Are you serious?" she asked faintly.

"Why not?" He was all reason, not a sign of emotion. "If you're worried, I give you my word I won't try to change your mind."

Was there a slight emphasis on the word try? She couldn't be sure. "It's not a good idea," she protested, visibly weakening. She was a fool for even considering it.

"Dinner, that's all I'm asking," he offered persuasively.

"Promise?"

He nodded, his eyes steady on hers. "Nothing more."

Unable to help herself, she agreed.

"Seven o'clock?"

She nodded. She felt rather than saw his relief at her acceptance. As he walked away she wondered if she had imagined the triumphant flash she had surprised in his eyes. She knew she was a fool to accept his company, but she couldn't deny herself this one final moment. Even the risk of ending up in his bed didn't deter her. She suspected the date was another ploy to influence her, but even that didn't matter. She knew her decision was the right one for her and she had faith in her own ability to stick to it.

* * *

Summer reached into her closet and removed the plastic-protected dress she had purchased on a whim the week after her return from the Bahamas. She had felt so down she had treated herself to a completely feminine shopping spree. This was the result.

She surveyed the soft cream silk without its concealing wrapper in satisfaction. On the hanger it was nothing much to see, but on . . . The deep vee plunge hugged her breasts perfectly, the lightly shirred skirt gathered around her narrow waist to froth to a stop just below her knees. The color was an exquisite foil for her honey tan, or at least that's what the salesgirl had assured her when she bought it. With the addition of a narrow gold belt, the matching high heels and evening bag she had purchased especially for it, she knew she had never looked better. The final touch was a delicate gold pendant locket on a fairy-light chain, a gift from Gussie on her twenty-first birthday.

She checked her appearance in the mirror one last time. The vision that stared back at her was reassuring. Every inch of her was sleek and pampered from the top of her shimmering curls to the tips of her nylon-clad toes. She slipped the feathery crocheted stole over her bare arms as protection against the evening chill. Although it was still in the warm seventies in the day, the nights had begun to get cooler.

She heard the door chimes and felt the first stirrings of excitement or panic, she wasn't quite sure which. She listened to Brandon's deep voice as he greeted her sister-in-law. She waited for Gussie's knock before she opened the door.

When she stepped into the lighted hall she stared straight into Brandon's eyes. Beside her she was conscious of Gussie's gasp of surprise, but it was his reaction she sought.

It was all she could have hoped for. She watched the stunned expression with inward amusement, saw the sea-green eyes kindle with admiration and desire. Somehow in the back of her mind she realized the battle was not over, the last gun was still unfired.

She smiled, a slow, deliberately sexy invitation. She had not consciously planned this evening, but suddenly she knew she wanted it. She loved Brandon and she was going to fight to get him, but on her terms. If she lost, then at least she knew she had tried.

Brandon reacted to her provocation with narrowed eyes. She could almost see his brain racing for a reason for her change toward him.

Summer stepped forward, for once the leader in their unusual relationship. "I hope I didn't keep you waiting," she murmured in a husky tone, completely ignoring Gussie's presence.

Brandon had recovered his surprise enough to take the hand she held out. "Not at all." He used his hold to draw her into his arms for a kiss. As kisses go it was extremely brief, but both of them were conscious of a waiting quality.

Summer acted on instinct alone. She had never in her life set out to captivate a man, so she had no experience to draw from. What she did have was an overwhelming love for this tall, stubborn bachelor. She was banking that his professed feelings for her were as deep as her own. She refused to believe they weren't. They had survived a separation and his not inconsiderable determination to kill them. It had to be more than desire even if he wouldn't admit it. Although she didn't intend to trick him, she sure as the devil was going to show him what he was missing. She had declared her love and it had gotten her nowhere, so . . .

"Are you ready?" Brandon asked, taking her arm.

She nodded turning to Gussie. She saw the shock in

the older woman's eyes, but she also saw understanding.

"I won't wait up," Gussie said. "Have a nice time."

"Do you suppose she meant it?" Brandon asked as he slid into the driver's seat of his rented Mercedes.

Summer stared at him in the dim light. "Is there a reason why she wouldn't?"

"Not that I know of," he replied, starting the engine. "I have reservations for us at the Ebb Tide. It's supposed to have a good band."

She agreed, amused at the conventional remark. It took the better part of dinner for Brandon to finally make something more than polite conversation.

Summer had been thoroughly enjoying her new role as femme fatale. She had gazed worshipfully into his eyes as he spoke until he had stopped in midsentence, had sipped ever so slowly from her wineglass, then lowered it, leaving a thin film of liquid on her lips that she carefully removed with the tip of her tongue. That trick she had seen in a movie once and had howled over the poor hero's besotted expression. While Brandon didn't look quite that bad, he certainly wasn't his usual cool self.

"Would you mind telling me exactly what you're playing at?" he demanded when the waiter had removed their empty plates.

Summer was all innocence, her honey eyes never so soft. "Why, Brandon, don't you like the new me?" she asked at her most provocative. "I thought this was the way all mistresses behaved toward their protectors."

Brandon glared at her, hating the old-fashioned name on her lips. Was she trying to tell him she had changed her mind? "You mean you're going to accept my offer?" His voice was an angry whisper, indicating no pleasure at the possibility.

She tipped her head to one side, lowering her lashes

180

until she could just make out his expression. She didn't dare let him see the laughter she felt. For a man who so ardently pleaded with her to live with him, he didn't look a bit pleased. In fact, he appeared ready to commit murder—hers!

"A lady can always change her mind," she admitted slowly.

Brandon stared at her intently. What the hell was she playing at now?

The waiter approached. "Will that be all, sir?"

Brandon looked up, barely masking his rising temper. "Just the check," he ordered curtly.

"Are we leaving?" Summer asked.

"We are," he stated in a tone that dared her to object. "We're going to my hotel suite. You and I are going to have a little talk." He waited for her refusal. He didn't get one.

"Fine," she agreed, rising to her feet. "I don't suppose you have any brandy, do you?"

He took her arm, his tight hold indicative of the rein he was keeping on his temper. "Summer, if you say one more word, I swear . . ."

Prudently Summer ceased tormenting. While he drove she contented herself with remembering his angry surprise at her apparent reversal. Surely that meant something. After all, only a few hours before he had said it was what he wanted.

As he swiftly escorted her to his suite, Summer blessed the fact she wasn't in a tight skirt or she never would have kept pace with Brandon's long strides. Not that she had much choice, since he had a death grip on her arm.

He swung her into the room, releasing her abruptly when he slammed the door shut. She stared at him as he advanced to where she stood rooted in the middle of the floor. His expression was thunderous.

If she had wanted to arouse him, she certainly had succeeded, if not in exactly the way she had anticipated.

"Now, suppose you tell me what's going on, and before you start, don't give me that innocent I-don't-know-what-you're-talking-about look." He raked his hand impatiently through his hair and tugged at the constricting tie around his neck. "This has been, without a doubt, the worst evening I've had in the past three weeks. Nothing has gone as I planned."

"Planned?" Summer asked, alert to the frustration in his tone. Until then she had allowed him to give rein to his temper, but now she wanted an explanation. "What do you mean, planned?" She didn't miss the light flush that crept up his neck. Suddenly her amusement at her spur-of-the-moment actions died. It didn't take much brainpower to guess what he had in mind. No wonder he was so mad. Her eyes shot sparks of molten lava.

"Before you explode, remember your own little act," he warned, well aware she had put two and two together. "I'm not denying I intended to seduce you if I could, but that's all."

"All?" she raged. "Seduce? In a pig's eye! I wouldn't get in bed with you, you pompous, conceited tyrant, if you were the last male on earth."

"Oh, really. Then what was little Miss Sexpot aiming for over dinner?" he roared back in retaliation. "It was like watching a rerun of an old movie."

They faced each other across a foot of plush carpet, two combatants equal in strength but so different in build.

Summer glared at him, a stare he returned in full measure.

"And don't call me tyrant again. I may deserve several names in our relationship, but not that one," he grated through gritted teeth.

Summer couldn't help it—she started to giggle. He

looked so incensed over her expression. Once she began, she couldn't stop. She collapsed onto a nearby sofa, the tears streaming unchecked down her cheeks.

"Are you laughing at me?" he demanded, coming over to tower over her. "Because if you are, I'll tan your hide."

She looked up at him. "Not at you, at both of us," she answered between giggles.

Suddenly the humor of it struck him and he chuckled. "My God, we sound like eight-year-olds," he admitted, dropping into the empty space beside her.

She nodded. "Shannon and Eric couldn't have done it better."

"Don't tell me. Her latest heartthrob? Is he good looking?"

"Nope," she smiled into his beloved face. "Red hair, freckles, all arms and legs."

Brandon grimaced. "What does she see in him?"

Summer shrugged. "What any woman sees in a man. Looks don't really matter, it's how he makes you feel." Suddenly the conversation was serious.

He searched her face, making no move to touch her. "And how do I make you feel?"

He saw the hesitation in her expression, the wary look in the tawny pools. "Shall I tell you what you do to me? You delight my eyes. Fill me with desire to possess you. Yet I want to protect you, keep you safe. You make me lose my temper quicker than anyone I know, but you make me laugh."

Summer reached out to trace the clean lines and planes of his face. She stared deep into his sea-colored eyes. He had come so close to saying those all-important words—words that would unlock the torrent of love inside her, only barely held in check.

He captured her hand, holding it across his cheek. She could feel the faint prickle of his beard beneath her palm. "I need you," he murmured in a deep rumble. "Stay with me tonight."

For a moment she almost said no, then the love she could no longer restrain took away her will to resist. Tomorrow was for goodbye, tonight was for memory. She nodded.

He rose, still holding her hand. He pulled her to her feet, their bodies pressed intimately together before he bent to slide an arm under her knees to lift her against his chest.

He carried her into the bedroom and gently laid her on the satin coverlet. He strode across to the wide sliding glass doors leading to a terrace and pushed them open.

Summer watched curiously. The sound of the muted roar of the ocean filled the room. She understood and she smiled. The moonlight reflected across them both just as it had that night.

He came to her, shedding his coat and unbuttoning his shirt. She could see the fire in his eyes as he leaned over her.

At first there were no words between them, their touches speaking of their mutual need. Clothes dropped soundlessly to the floor beside the bed until Summer lay naked against Brandon's warm, bare skin.

"I had forgotten how exquisite you are," he murmured, his hands traveling slowly over her slender contours. He raised on one elbow until he could see her expression. "You know I want you, golden eyes, but I'm beginning to see I need you. It can't be goodbye for us. I won't let it."

Summer shook her head, a sadness entering her eyes. "Better now, Brandon, than later. You know I haven't changed my mind."

"Your act was all a game earlier, wasn't it?" he asked, knowing the answer even as she nodded. "Why?"

"You wanted a mistress and I gave you what you asked for. I wanted to see your reaction. Why were you angry?" she asked, voicing a question of her own. She saw the surprise on his face as she gave a name to his feelings.

"I don't know for sure," he began hesitantly. "I think I finally saw what I was asking of you."

She waited, her heart in her eyes. Please let him love me, she begged silently. Let him say it.

"You are so sure you love me, but I'm not sure I know what love is anymore. I've never thought about the commitment you once described." He stared at her, willing her to understand what he barely understood himself.

Summer recognized the gulf between them more clearly than ever. The urge to reach out for him was undeniable. As she held up her arms he moved into her embrace, pillowing his head on her bare breast. She absorbed the beloved weight of him, wrapping him protectively in her arms. For a long moment he stayed still against her; then she felt a deep sigh ripple through him as though he had won a long fight.

"I love you."

The words were barely audible, but she heard the final commitment, the ultimate capitulation. Shock held her speechless.

His voice was muffled against her breast. "I didn't want to, I fought it and you, but I didn't kill it. Instead, it's swallowing me. I could leave here tomorrow and live, but there would be no joy in it. All the time I was away I saw your face in my mind. I don't just want an image, I want you! Marry me." He raised his head, an almost humble look in his eyes.

"Are you sure?" she asked, a desperate hope in her heart.

"Yes. Even if I didn't plan it this way."

She smiled, remembering the different plans they had started the evening with. The answering grin on his face dispelled her last doubt.

Her reply was lost in the searing hunger of his kiss. "I thought you would never ask," she whispered, feeling the last barriers to their life together slip away like the morning mist over the sea.

Silhouette Desire
15-Day Trial Offer
A new romance series that explores contemporary relationships in exciting detail

Six Silhouette Desire romances, free for 15 days!
We'll send you six new Silhouette Desire romances to look over for 15 days, absolutely free! If you decide not to keep the books, return them and owe nothing.

Six books a month, free home delivery. If you like Silhouette Desire romances as much as we think you will, keep them and return your payment with the invoice. Then we will send you six new books every month to preview, just as soon as they are published. You pay only for the books you decide to keep, and you never pay postage and handling.

YOU'LL BE SWEPT AWAY
WITH SILHOUETTE DESIRE

$1.75 each

1 ☐ CORPORATE AFFAIR
James

2 ☐ LOVE'S SILVER WEB
Monet

3 ☐ WISE FOLLY
Clay

4 ☐ KISS AND TELL
Carey

5 ☐ WHEN LAST WE LOVED
Baker

6 ☐ A FRENCHMAN'S KISS
Mallory

7 ☐ NOT EVEN FOR LOVE
St. Claire

8 ☐ MAKE NO PROMISES
Dee

9 ☐ MOMENT IN TIME
Simms

10 ☐ WHENEVER I LOVE YOU
Smith

$1.95 each

11 ☐ VELVET TOUCH
James

12 ☐ THE COWBOY AND THE
LADY   Palmer

13 ☐ COME BACK, MY LOVE
Wallace

14 ☐ BLANKET OF STARS
Valley

15 ☐ SWEET BONDAGE
Vernon

16 ☐ DREAM COME TRUE
Major

17 ☐ OF PASSION BORN
Simms

18 ☐ SECOND HARVEST
Ross

19 ☐ LOVER IN PURSUIT
James

20 ☐ KING OF DIAMONDS
Allison

21 ☐ LOVE INTHE CHINA SEA
Baker

22 ☐ BITTERSWEET IN BERN
Durant

23 ☐ CONSTANT STRANGER
Sunshine

24 ☐ SHARED MOMENTS
Baxter

25 ☐ RENAISSANCE MAN
James

26 ☐ SEPTEMBER MORNING
Palmer

27 ☐ ON WINGS OF NIGHT
Conrad

28 ☐ PASSIONATE JOURNEY
Lovan

29 ☐ ENCHANTED DESERT
Michelle

30 ☐ PAST FORGETTING
Lind

31 ☐ RECKLESS PASSION
James

32 ☐ YESTERDAY'S DREAMS
Clay

***LOOK FOR <u>ONE NIGHT'S DECEPTION</u>
BY KATHRYN MALLORY
AVAILABLE IN APRIL AND
<u>ALL THE NIGHT LONG</u>
BY SUZANNE SIMMS IN MAY.***

Silhouette Desire

Coming Next Month

Affair Of Honor by Stephanie James

When Ryder Sterne held her in his embrace, Philosophy professor Brenna Llewellyn almost forgot why she was at the mountain retreat, and soon found herself abandoning all logic for love.

Friends And Lovers by Diana Palmer

They were close friends, but now Madeline found that John's touch was somehow different. It ignited a passion in her that led them to discover a whole new closeness.

Shadow Of The Mountain by Pamela Lind

Deke Jordan had rights and could lay equal claim to Shelley Grant's small mining company. But Shelley didn't expect him to stake a claim on her with kisses she fought—but couldn't resist.

Embers Of The Sun by Raye Morgan

Artist Charla Evans came to Japan to study raku pottery—and to escape an unhappy love. But then she met tycoon Stephen Conners and realized she couldn't live for art alone!

Winter Lady by Janet Joyce

America's heartthrob Devlin Paige saved Raine Morgan when he rescued her on the ski slopes in Minnesota's desolate hills . . . but he left Raine burning with a reckless passion she couldn't escape.

If Ever You Need Me by Paula Fulford

When Julia Somers stepped off the stage in triumph, producer Roy Allison offered her a star-making role . . . and more. But could love be real in his celluloid world?

Get 6 new Silhouette Special Editions every month for a 15-day FREE trial!

Free Home Delivery, Free Previews, Free Bonus Books. Silhouette Special Editions are a new kind of romance novel. These are big, powerful stories that will capture your imagination. They're longer, with fully developed characters and intricate plots that will hold you spellbound from the first page to the very last.

Each month we will send you six exciting *new* Silhouette Special Editions, just as soon as they are published. If you enjoy them as much as we think you will, pay the invoice enclosed with your shipment. **They're delivered right to your door with never a charge for postage or handling, and there's no obligation to buy anything at any time.** To start receiving Silhouette Special Editions regularly, mail the coupon below today.

Silhouette Special Edition

READERS' COMMENTS ON SILHOUETTE DESIRES